DEAR COMMITTEE MEMBERS

DEAR COMMITTEE MEMBERS

Julie Schumacher

The Friday Project
An imprint of HarperCollinsPublishers
1 London Bridge Street
London SE1 9GF
www.harpercollins.co.uk

First published by Doubleday in 2014
First published in Great Britain by The Friday Project in 2014

This paperback edition 2015

Copyright © Julie Schumacher 2014

Julie Schumacher asserts the moral right to be identified as the author of this work
A catalogue record for this book is available from the British Library

ISBN: 978-0-00-812088-7

Jacket design by We Are Laura

Printed and bound in Great Britain by Clays Ltd, St Ives plc

MIX
Paper from
responsible sources
FSC™ C007454

FSC™ is a non-profit international organisation established to promote
the responsible management of the world's forests. Products carrying the
FSC label are independently certified to assure consumers that they come
from forests that are managed to meet the social, economic and
ecological needs of present and future generations,
and other controlled sources.

Find out more about HarperCollins and the environment at
www.harpercollins.co.uk/green

To my students

DEAR COMMITTEE MEMBERS

September 3, 2009
Bentham Literary Residency Program
P.O. Box 1572
Bentham, ME 04976

Dear Committee Members,

Over the past twenty-odd years I've recommended god only knows how many talented candidates for the Bentham January residency—that enviable literary oasis in the woods south of Skowhegan: the solitude, the pristine cabins, the artistic camaraderie, and those exquisite hand-delivered satchels of apples and cheese . . . Well, you can scratch all prior nominees and pretenders from your mailing lists, because none is as provocative or as promising as Darren Browles.

Mr. Browles is my advisee; he's taken two of my workshops, and his novel-in-progress, a retelling of Melville's *Bartleby* (but in which the eponymous character is hired to keep the books at a brothel, circa 1960, just outside Las Vegas), is both tender satire and blistering adaptation/homage. In brief: this tour de force is witty, incisive, original, brutally sophisticated, erotic. You don't need me to summarize it—you'll have received his two opening chapters. My agent, Ken Doyle, is apprised of the project and is gnashing his pearly incisors in the hope of receiving the completed manuscript soon. Any additional perks or funding you can provide for Browles during the residency will be appreciated; he's likely to be wooed by editors all over New York.

A personal aside: I was very sorry to hear of Mike's death. He was a terrific director, and I always enjoyed talking to him in the row of blue rocking chairs out on the porch during the occasions (too rare!) when I was able to escape my academic duties here in the Midwest and accept his invitations to Bentham. He'll be terribly hard to replace. Whoever tries to step into them will find he wore sizeable, generous shoes.

In sadness but looking to the future,
Jason T. Fitger
Professor of Creative Writing and English
Department of English
Payne University

Dear Ted,

Your memo of August 30 requests that we on the English faculty recommend some luckless colleague for the position of director of graduate studies. (You may have been surprised to find this position vacant upon your assumption of the chairship last month—if so, trust me, you will encounter many such surprises here.)

A quick aside, Ted: god knows what enticements were employed during the heat of summer to persuade you—a sociologist!—to accept the position of chair in a department not your own, an academic unit whose reputation for eccentricity and discord has inspired the upper echelon to punish us by withholding favors as if from a six-year-old at a birthday party: *No raises or research funds for you, you ungovernable rascals! And no fudge before dinner!* Perhaps, as the subject of a sociological study, you will find the problem of our dwindling status intriguing.

To the matter at hand: though English has traditionally been a largish department, you will find there are very few viable candidates capable of assuming the mantle of DGS. In fact, if I were a betting man, I'd wager that only 10 percent of the English instruction list will answer your call for nominations. Why? First, because more than a third of our faculty now consists of temporary (adjunct) instructors who creep into the building under cover of darkness to teach their graveyard shifts of freshman comp; they are not eligible to vote or to serve. Second, because the remaining two-thirds of the faculty, bearing the scars of disenfranchisement and long-term abuse, are busy tending to personal grudges like scraps of carrion on which they gnaw in the gloom of their offices. Long story short: your options aren't pretty.

After subtracting the names of those who are on leave or close to retirement, and those already serving in the killing fields of administration, you will probably be forced to choose between Franklin Kentrell (NO: spend five consecutive minutes with him and you will understand why); Jennifer Brown-Wilson (a whipping girl for the theory faction—already terrorized, she will decline); Albert Tyne (under no circumstances should you enter his office without several days' warning—more on this later); Donna Lovejoy (poor overworked creature—I hereby nominate her [anonymously please] with this letter); and me. You'll soon find that I make myself unpleasant enough to be safe from nomination.

Enfin: Lovejoy will sag under this additional burden, but she will perform.

Ted, in your memo you referred briefly, also, to the need for faculty forbearance during what we were initially told would be the "remodeling" of the second floor for the benefit of our colleagues in the Economics Department.* I'm not sure that you noticed, but the Econ faculty were, in early August, evacuated from the building—as if they'd been notified, *sotto voce,* of an oncoming plague. Not so the faculty in English. With the exception of a few individuals both fleet of foot and quick-witted enough to claim status as asthmatics, we have been Left Behind, almost biblically, expected to begin our classes and meet with students while bulldozers snarl at the door. Yesterday afternoon during my Multicultural American Literature class, I watched a wrecking ball swinging like a hypnotist's watch just past the window. While I am relieved to know that the economists—delicate creatures!—have been safely installed in a wing of the new geology building where their physical comfort and aesthetic needs can be addressed, those of us who remain as castaways here in Willard Hall risk not only deafness but mutation: as of next week we have been instructed to keep our windows tightly closed due to "particulate matter"—but my office window (here's the amusing part, Ted) no longer shuts. One theory here: the deanery is annoyed with our requests for parity and, weary of waiting for us to retire, has decided to kill us. Let the academic year begin!

Cordially and with a hearty welcome to the madhouse,
Jay

* Under whose aegis was it decided that Economics and English should share a building? Were criteria other than the alphabet considered?

Dear Ms. Ingersol,

This letter is intended to bolster the application to Wexler Foods of my former student John Leszczynski, who completed the Junior/Senior Creative Writing Workshop three months ago. Mr. Leszczynski received a final grade of B, primarily on the basis of an eleven-page short story about an inebriated man who tumbles into a cave and surfaces from an alcoholic stupor to find that a tentacled monster—a sort of fanged and copiously salivating octopus, if memory serves—is gnawing through the flesh of his lower legs, the monster's spittle burbling ever closer to the victim's groin. Though chaotic and improbable even within the fantasy/horror genre, the story was solidly constructed: dialogue consisted primarily of agonized groans and screaming; the chronology was relentlessly clear.

Mr. Leszczynski attended class faithfully, arriving on time, and rarely succumbed to the undergraduate impulse to check his cell phone for messages or relentlessly zip and unzip his backpack in the final minutes of class.

Whether punctuality and an enthusiasm for flesh-eating cephalopods are the main attributes of the ideal Wexler employee I have no idea, but Mr. Leszczynski is an affable young man, reliable in his habits, and reasonably bright.

You might start him off in produce, rather than seafood or meats.

Whimsically,
Jason T. Fitger, Professor of Creative Writing/English
Payne University

Dear Ted:

You've asked me to write a letter seconding the nomination of Franklin Kentrell for Payne's coveted Davidson Chair. I assume Kentrell is behind this request; no sane person would nominate a man whose only recent publications consist of personal genealogical material and who wears visible sock garters in class—all he lacks is a white tin basin to resemble a nineteenth-century barber.

But if you want me to endorse his nomination in order to keep him quiet and away from your office (you will find him as persistent and maddening as a fly), you may excerpt the following sentences and affix my name to them: "Professor Franklin Kentrell has a singular mind and a unique approach to the discipline. He is sui generis. The Davidson Chair has never seen his like before."

A word on the call for official, written letters of recommendation, Ted: I hope for the sake of all concerned you will cut back on these as much as possible. The LOR has become a rampant absurdity, usurping the place of the quick consultation

8

and the two-minute phone call—not to mention the teaching and research that faculty were supposedly hired to perform. I haven't published a novel in six years; instead, I fill my departmental hours casting words of praise into the bureaucratic abyss. On multiple occasions, serving on awards committees, I was actually required to write LORs to myself.

Keeping my temper under wraps for the present,
Jay

P.S.: I couldn't help but notice, following the departure of the economists, that our Tech Help office has been largely vacated as well, a single employee—the appropriately named Mr. Duffy Napp—left behind to respond to faculty requests for computer assistance. This surly somnambulist rarely deigns to answer the most basic of questions and treats with exhausted dismay any individual who is not a specialist in computer arcana. Might it be possible to exchange "the Napper" for someone more civil and less lethargic?

P.P.S.: Thank you for your attention to my office window, which now closes, but due to an impressive crack in the frame—presumably caused by the earsplitting construction on the second floor—rainwater is trickling merrily down the *inside* of the glass and, as I type these words, entering the rusted slats of the heater. You might want to send someone to take a look.

September 17, 2009
Bentham Literary Residency Program
P.O. Box 1572
Bentham, ME 04976

Dear Overworked Committee Members,

Ms. Vivian Zelles has asked me—three days before your application deadline—to recommend her to your January residency program at Bentham, and herewith I oblige.

Ms. Zelles is an apt and diligent writer, a second-year graduate student in comparative literature currently enrolled, as a sort of academic stowaway, in my fiction workshop. Her project, to date, consists of a series of short, linked narratives on the subject of childhood and family and female relationships, romantic and otherwise. The work is young and presumably autobiographical; still, one can discern a spark of energy here and there in the occasional quirks of the tone. Ms. Zelles is not among the top tier of students I generally prefer to send your way (e.g., Darren Browles—see my LOR of September 3), but in the coming year or two her work may mature.

Feel free to contact me for further information via phone or e-mail. And forgive the brevity of this letter: I do believe that student writing speaks for itself, and though the academic year has just started I fear I am already losing the never-ending battle to catch up with the recommendations requested of me. Suffice it to say that the LOR has usurped the place of my own work, now adorned with cobwebs and dust in a remote corner of my office.

Continuing to wish you well with the search for a new director,
Jason T. Fitger
Professor of Creative Writing and English
Payne University

September 22, 2009
Payne University Law School Admissions
c/o Janet Matthias (aka Janet Matthias-Fitger)
17 Pitlinger Hall

Dear Admissions Committee Members—and Janet:

This letter recommends Melanie deRueda for admission to the law school on the well-heeled side of this campus. I've known Ms. deRueda for eleven minutes, ten of which were spent in a fruitless attempt to explain to her that I write letters of recommendation only for students who have signed up for and completed one of my classes. This young woman is certainly tenacious, if that's what you're looking for. A transfer student, she appears to be suffering under the delusion that a recommendation from any random faculty member within our august institution will be the key to her application's success.

Janet: I know your committees aren't reading these blasted LORs—under the influence of our final martini in August you told me as much. (I wish I had an ex-wife like you in every department; over in the Fellowship Office, the formerly benevolent Carole continues to maintain an icy distance. I should think her decision to quit our relationship would have filled her with a cheerful burst of self-esteem, but she apparently views the end of our three years together in a different light.)

Ms. deRueda claims to be sending her transcripts and LSAT scores at the end of the week. God help you—this is your shot across the bow—should you admit her.

Still affectionately your one-time husband,
Jay

P.S.: I've heard a rumor that Eleanor—yes, *that* Eleanor, from the Seminar—is a finalist for the directorship at Bentham. You got back in touch with her despite her denouncements of me; do you have any intel?

P.P.S.: A correction: you got back in touch with Eleanor *because* she denounced me. I remember you quoting what she said when I published *Transfer of Affection:* that I was an egotist prone to repeating his most fatal mistakes. I'll admit to the egotism—which is undeniable—but I'd like to think that, after fourteen years of marriage, you knew me better than Eleanor did. We were happy for some of those fourteen years, especially before *Transfer;* why shouldn't I believe that you were right about me, too?

September 30, 2009
Field-Bantry College of Government and Public Affairs
Office of Graduate Admissions
447 Peck Hall
Whaylon, PA 19522

Dear Committee Members,

This letter recommends Ms. Stella Castle to your graduate institution in the field of public policy. And to begin this recommendation on the proper footing: no, I will not fill out the inane computerized form that is intended to precede or supplant this letter; ranking a student according to his or her placement among the "top 10 percent," "top 2 percent," or "top 0.000001 percent" is pointless and absurd. No faculty member will rank any student, no matter how severely lacking in ability or reason, below "top 10 percent." This would be tantamount to describing the candidate in question as a witless beast. A human being and his or her caliber, intellect, character, and promise are not reducible to a check mark in a box. Faced with a reductionist formula such as yours, I despair for the future, consoling myself with the thought that I and others of my generation, with its archaic modes of discourse, won't live to see the barren cyberworld the authors of your recommendation form are determined to create.

Ms. Castle was a student in my American Literature Survey a year ago. She is a serious-minded young woman whose analytical skills and arguments demonstrate a subtle acumen. More than once, in class, I saw her politely demolish another student's interpretation of a work of literature by asking a series of seemingly innocent but progressively incisive questions. Perhaps oddly, I remember thinking of Ms. Castle as a highly articulate snake: sliding gracefully into an argument, speaking in lucid, sibilant phrases (she endows the letter *S* with the faintest suggestion of a whistle), and then striking to inject the requisite venom.

Ms. Castle wrote a final, exquisite essay on Willa Cather's *The Professor's House*—probably a lost tome as far as you policy wonks are concerned—on which she received a well-deserved A.

I recommend her to you very highly. She is excellent. She will not fit into any of your miniature boxes. I will now insert this letter in an envelope, maintaining a paper copy for safekeeping in a drawer by my desk, after which I will take a short stroll to the picturesque blue mailbox on the corner, opening its creaking rectangular metal mouth and dropping the envelope within.

Trusting the U.S. Postal Service to deliver this missive to you in a timely fashion, I am

J. Fitger

Professor and Upholder of the Ancient Flame

Payne University

Dear Eleanor,

Congratulations on the ~~dictatorship~~ (haha!) directorship! Well done! Who would have guessed, twenty-some years ago when we were living on pizza crust and challenging the poets to recitation games[*] in the student lounge, that you'd be in charge of Bentham and I'd be sending you my best and my brightest? In any case, kudos. Toiling for decades through the murk of the corporate world and then the nonprofits must not have been easy, but I'm sure you've garnered some valuable expertise.

I'm appealing to you directly to recommend in emphatic terms an advisee and student, Darren Browles. I'm aware that your committees are beavering through mountains of applications

---

[*] They usually beat us, of course, but we were reading several novels a week, while their coursework fit comfortably on a single folded sheet of loose-leaf in a pants pocket. Ah, the strenuous life of the poet: he snips a few adjectives from the daily paper, tapes them in a spiral to his office door, and calls the workweek done.

for the January residencies, and while winter seems distant at this time of year (as I type this letter, shirtless undergrads are frolicking on the quad), I assume that decisions will be made under pressure, and soon. Hence this additional recommendation on behalf of Mr. Browles, who shuffled into my office this morning, dejected, to tell me he will be taking a leave of absence this spring for financial reasons. He should have had a teaching assistantship, but our graduate program has been put on the chopping block, all funds to be diverted to the technical fields.

Eleanor: If Bentham could offer Browles a residency not only for the January term but through spring, I'm confident he can finish his manuscript, *Accountant in a Bordello*, and then his degree. As a prose stylist, Browles is a high-wire performer— but if he loses momentum . . . We've both been there, Eleanor: I have a desk half full of projects that, lacking time and attention, have succumbed to these small, pitiful deaths; and I'm sure your slender volume of stories (Janet bought two copies the week it came out) would have been followed by a novel, had your schedule allowed. The bottom line: I'm making a personal appeal, for the sake of our years together in the Seminar, that you arrange to float Browles financially at Bentham through winter and spring.

Anticipating a positive reply,
Jay

P.S.: I'm aware that you and Janet reestablished a correspondence during the period of our marriage's dissolution and I
hope any vitriol she might have expressed won't compromise
my professional relationship with you. (In case you're waiting
for me to acknowledge that I behaved like an ass, I hereby
admit it; but Janet has forgiven me: we see each other twice a
year on what was our wedding anniversary, in August, and on
the date when we signed our divorce agreement, February 3.)
There's no changing the past; we can only stumble haphazardly
forward. I appreciate any particular attention you can devote
to Darren Browles.

Dear Dean Hinckler,

I write in support of my colleague, Assistant Professor Lance West, regarding his nomination for the university's Campiello Undergraduate Advising and Service Award. West is a solid junior scholar; more apropos of the current occasion, he has served for three of his four short years at Payne in administration, directing the undergraduate writing center and the much contested/maligned composition program. (No reasonable person outside a university would believe the teaching of composition to be controversial, but of course it is.) Professor West has an open-door policy and a rapport—one is almost tempted to call it a flair—with the incoming freshmen. He has worked hard, he has done what was asked of him, and—in the wake of the deliberate gutting of the liberal arts, English in particular, in favor of the technological sciences—he has held together the tattered scraps of the literature and writing programs, which the faceless gremlins in your office have condemned to indigence and ruin.

Furthermore, West is not yet jaded or cynical; a former Eagle Scout, he maintains a "team spirit" approach to the institution. Before construction forced us to seal ourselves into our offices like agoraphobic strangers in a cut-rate motel, I could frequently hear, across the hall and three doors down, in West's office, the contented chatter of freshmen being persuaded that clarity of expression might be achievable as well as worthwhile.

Only by rewarding West and others of his happy ilk, and perhaps by killing off senior faculty, myself included, will it be possible for that elusive and almost mythical beast—collegiality—to prevail. (You may have thought that plunging us into receivership and imposing an outsider as our chair would serve to unite us, but Boti is sadly out of his element; he wanders the halls, bewildered, with a soiled bandanna affixed to his face[*] like a madman descending into a dream.)

Other LORs cascading onto your desk like autumn leaves may suggest that the Campiello Award, associated with a modest financial settlement and a plaque on which the administration does its best to spell the awardee's name correctly, should be given to a colleague more senior than West. This is shortsighted thinking. West is not yet entrenched, and because of the caliber of his scholarship and his regular presence at the requisite conferences, he is rapidly making a name for himself. If we don't engage in an aggressive effort to retain him, other (more presti-

---

[*] We are inhaling more dust over here in Willard Hall than an average coal miner—please send a backup supply of medical masks ASAP.

gious) institutions will poach. West is unprepossessing—but he is also a striver. Put a ladder in front of him and he will eagerly climb it. So much intellectual will and ambition! I confess: at this point of my career, that sort of enthusiasm fatigues me. The role that is left to me is to stand in the patronizing shadow of my younger and more aspiring colleagues and *push*. Up the chimney with you, and don't get soot on your knickers along the way!

Those of you in the superior ranks of the Land of Red Tape would do well to watch your backs: if West hasn't yet fled the institution, he'll have one of your jobs in a few short years.

With the customary respect and a nod of deference,
Jason Fitger, Professor/Hazardous Materials Specialist
Willard Hall

October 16, 2009
Avengers Paintball, Inc.
1778 Industrial Blvd.
Lakeville, MN 55044

Esteemed Avengers,

This letter recommends Mr. Allen Trent for a position at your paintball emporium. Mr. Trent received a C– in my expository writing class last spring, which—given my newly streamlined and increasingly generous grading criteria—is quite the accomplishment. His final project consisted of a ten-page autobiographical essay on the topic of his own rageful impulses and his (often futile) attempts to control them. He cited his dentist and his roommate as primary sources.

Consider this missive a testament to Mr. Trent's preparedness for the work your place of business undoubtedly has in store.

Hoping to maintain a distance of at least one hundred yards,
Jason T. Fitger
Professor of Creative Writing and English
Payne University ("Teach 'til It Hurts")

(My all-inclusive calendar invites me to celebrate Diwali today)
Ken Doyle
Hautman and Doyle Literary Agency
141 West 27th Street
New York, NY 10001

Dear Ken—

Business first: I'm writing on behalf of a student—you remember students from our Seminar days, I'm sure—Darren Browles, who is currently putting the finishing touches on a powerhouse work of fiction: a debut novel, an excerpt from which, if I manage to knock some sense into his rocky skull, will be on your desk next week.

Accountant in a Bordello is a shattering reinterpretation of *Bartleby:* the main character, tight-lipped introvert Herman Crown, is an accountant at one of the biggest legal whorehouses in the state of Nevada, spending his days tallying expenses, passing up opportunities at wealth and advancement, eschewing friendships, and generally maintaining, amidst the titillating hubbub of his surroundings, a dispassionate isolation, an existential solitude. The prose—at one moment profoundly spare, the next moment rococo—is entirely his own; Ken, it's like nothing you've ever seen. I urged him to send you the entire manuscript (which, admittedly, should be trimmed, at five-hundred-plus pages), but Browles is cautious and will probably submit only the first several chapters. As his advisor, even I haven't read the book straight through—Browles hands me a chunk, scuttles back to his hidey-hole to revise, then reappears with another. Ken: take him on. This is a book that—after a little light housework—should garner multiple bids at auction. And a healthy advance will allow Browles to trim and to work with a top-notch editor on the final version.

On the personal side: I'm sorry about the tone of the conversation we had last year. *Transfer of Affection* didn't sell the way either of us had hoped (where did that pinhead in the *Inquirer* get off calling it an "embarrassment for both author and reviewer"?), but that was a blip, not a moratorium—and for you to hand the excerpt of my novel in progress to your assistant . . . Well, never mind. Water under the bridge and all that; I'm sure the twelve-year-old you assigned the task of evaluating my work did her utmost. In any case, I hope you won't let the memory of any previous quibbles prevent you from recognizing a phenomenon like Browles, who, I believe, will soon be enjoying some literary solitude at Bentham.

You've heard that Eleanor A. is now Bentham's director? Do you remember her throwing an apple core at me across the

Seminar table in HRH's class? She was ill-disposed toward me even before I wrote and published *Stain*. Here's hoping her directorial skills are better than her throwing arm.

Nostalgically,
Jay

Confidential Reference for LTZ39JN7 Jervana Natal

1. How long and in what capacity have you known the applicant?

Ms. Natal is a senior due to graduate in May of this coming year. I have known her for

Confidential Reference for LTZ39JN7 Jervana Natal

1. How long and in what capacity have you known the applicant?

I have known Ms. Natal for approximately eight weeks. She is a senior due to graduate in

Confidential Reference for LTZ39JN7 Jervana Natal

You have requested technological assistance regarding the submission of the above-named reference. Please describe the problem you are experiencing.

The problem I am experiencing is that every time I hit the fucking return key or try to indent a

Confidential Reference for LTZ39JN7 Jervana Natal

the fucking return key or try to indent or god forbid fit a coherent sentence into your fucking

October 23, 2009
Student Services/Fellowship Office
14 Gilbert Hall
Attn: The Gentle Carole Samarkind, Associate Director

Dear Carole:

This letter's purpose is to provide the usual gratuitous language recommending a student, one Gunnar Lang, for a work-study fellowship. Lang—a sophomore with a mop of blond dreadlocks erupting from the top of his head like the yellow coils of an excess brain—tells me that he has applied, unsuccessfully, for this same golden opportunity three times and that this is his final attempt to satisfy our university's endless requests for redundant documentation. He needs a minimum of eight to ten hours of work-study per week—preferably in the library rather than the slops of food service. Deny him the fellowship and he will undoubtedly turn his hand to something more lucrative, probably hawking illegal substances between the athletic facilities and the Pizza Barn.

I'll go ahead and point out the obvious: Lang's GPA is a respectable 3.4; he's on track, academically, despite a shift from psychology to English; and a ten-minute conversation with the subject himself reveals that he has bona fide thoughts and knows how to apportion them into relatively grammatical sentences. You should do yourself a favor and invent a reason to meet him. He's charming in a saucy, loose-limbed way, and his hair—his parents did right to name him Gunnar—is a phenomenon unto itself that I suspect you'll enjoy.

There: Lang has my stamp of approval and imprimatur. Now let me say how appreciative I am of the cordial professional-ism you've reestablished between us. I'm sure you know how profoundly I regret that boneheaded e-mail in August, and of course I don't blame you for cutting things off (though I wish you'd told me you'd be reclaiming the coffee machine, which was a gift, after all; I'm reminded of its absence every day by a circle of grime on the Formica).

Side note: I saw that you and Janet are both serving on the diversity committee.[*] Might that be . . . awkward? I do hope you won't sit next to each other. Even six years after our divorce, Janet considers herself an expert on the sub-ject of my many foibles, and she is often eager to share her questionable wisdom with others. Fair warning here, Carole: though smooth-spoken and polished, Janet is as cunning as a wolverine.

[*] I was barred from that committee myself; my filibuster last year (I argued that the arts are a form of diversity) was sadly characterized as "divisive."

28

Back to business. Please get the work-study fellowship for Lang and put him in the library, or even here in the department. He needs to acquaint himself with the nineteenth century before I let him loose in Donna Lovejoy's class.

Missing you (and missing my coffee),
J.

Dear Committee Members,

This letter recommends Vivian Zelles for admission to Payne University's medical school. Ms. Zelles is an excellent student, as will be obvious from her scores and transcripts. The recipient of an undergraduate double degree in biochemistry and music (enhanced by a minor in English), she is currently pursuing a master's in comparative literature while simultaneously composing a book-length novel/memoir, a coy mishmash of forms. She is a member of that rare breed whose feet are planted as firmly in the arts as in the sciences.

I have known Ms. Zelles for approximately nine months, in the context of two creative writing workshops. She is a fastidious and methodical stylist: one imagines her setting each word in place with a jeweler's loupe. Her ultimate plan, in applying to med school, may be to join the ranks of physician-writers who, not content to leave the pursuit of literary success to the starving artist, complement their million-dollar medical sala-

* You must have more fun with the name over there than we do.

ries with Random House contracts. (Move over, Gawande and Hosseini!)

I recommend Ms. Zelles to you with all the usual accolades these letters are expected to provide.

Yours on the underfunded wing of the campus,
Jay Fitger, Professor of Creative Writing and English
Author
Provocateur

October 29, 2009
Janet Matthias . . . Fitger
Payne University Law School—Admissions
17 Pitlinger Hall

Dear Law School Admissions Committee/Janet:

This letter recommends Vivian Zelles to your esteemed body. Ms. Zelles is an excellent student as will be obvious from her scores and transcripts. She is applying for a residency at Bentham and to Payne's medical school as well as the law school; whether this diffuse approach indicates a wide range of interests or some sort of chemical imbalance or illness, I haven't a clue.

I have known Ms. Zelles for approximately nine months. She sat in on my undergraduate workshop last spring—boggling the minds of the younger students with irrelevant theoretical asides—and is currently enrolled in what may be the last graduate-level fiction class ever taught at Payne. (I'm sure you read my screed last month in the campus rag.) Her work is meticulous but not very interesting. Moment of truth: personally, I don't care for Ms. Zelles, who may be ideally suited to law school. She is obviously brilliant, but I find her off-putting and a bit of a cipher. She has a mind like a bric-a-brac storehouse of facts: a surplus of content put to questionable use.

Janet: Your phone has been going straight to voice mail. Are you out of town? Please call. Eleanor has been stonewalling an advisee I've recommended to Bentham, and I wonder if she's talked to you. Good god, it's been twenty-two years since the Seminar. Yes, Reg admired my work. Yes, he helped me publish *Stain* and threw His Royal Weight behind the book. I didn't ask him to prefer my writing to yours or Troy's or Eleanor's or Ken's or even MTV's. (Who'd have thunk MTV would marry a vet and turn into a shrink?) But Eleanor is still carving voodoo dolls in my likeness. Are we going to spend the rest of our days in the shadow of H. Reginald Hanf and the Seminar, those few (admittedly powerful) years ever dogging our steps?

Fretfully, your former spouse,
Jay

P.S.: Thank you for *not* requiring that recommenders submit their letters via an online form. Though technically capable of e-mail, I remain leery, given the fiasco of my "reply all" message in August. (Carole says she is no longer angry, but—given that she requisitioned the coffee machine she bought for my birthday—it appears that her forgiveness is not yet complete.) Call me a Luddite, but I intend to resist for as long as possible the use of robotic fill-in-the-blank quantifiers for the intellectual attributes of human beings.

October 30, 2009
Theodore Boti, CEO
Department of English

Dear Ted,

This letter endorses the work-study application of Gunnar Lang, sophomore, who after months of heroic effort has been duly vetted by the Student Services/Fellowship staff, his one-page résumé grinding its weary way through the system and arriving at last for review in our department with six pounds of red tape clinging to its hem. One wonders which would be more difficult: to secure a minimum-wage job as an English Department undergraduate gofer or to obtain a passport and security clearance through the Middle East. If we give Lang ten hours a week to run errands and let us know when the copier is broken (it is broken at present; perhaps Lang could be persuaded to shave his head and don a monk's brown sackcloth and work as a scribe), he might have hope of making progress toward his degree.

By the by: I noticed in your departmental plan (I presume I'm the only person who has actually read the plan—you may as well have addressed it to me) that you intend to schedule two faculty meetings this year for the purpose of revising the department constitution. Two quick considerations here, Ted:

1. I wonder, during a time of fiscal, curricular, and architectural crisis, whether our top priority should be the pointless updating of a document no one will read;

2. Fair warning: As a body we tried, in a plenary/horror session when Sarah Lempert was chair, to revise the momentous founding document on which our department depends. We argued for weeks about the existence and then the location of a particular semicolon, two senior members of the faculty—true, one of them retired and left for rehab that same semester— abandoning the penultimate meeting in tears. (If you'd like to see it, I've been keeping a log of department meetings ranked according to level of trauma, with a 1 indicating mild contentiousness, a 3 signifying uncontrolled shouting, and a 5 leading to at least one nervous breakdown and/or immediate referral to the crisis center run by the Office of Mental Health.) I guarantee you: mention the word "constitution" and you'll have a 911 situation on your hands.

Thinking positively, and at your service as always—
Jay

P.S.: At the upcoming Assembly of Department Chairs meeting I hope you will raise the issue of hires for English and the defunding of our creative writing MA. The idea of graduate writing being defunded because of *expense* . . . Ted, faculty in Hutchinson Hall are decorating their million-dollar labs with hadron colliders, while we're told there's no money for a functioning chalkboard and a table and chairs. If Donna Lovejoy is up to it (I understand she went home yesterday with a work-related lung infection), you may want to bring her to the meeting with you: she witnessed last year's auto-da-fé and, given the recent sprinkler system malfunction in her office, will probably bring to the proceedings a sharpened perspective.

November 3, 2009
Anna Huston, Director
Annie's Nannies Child and Play Center
370 Shadow Pond Way
Cortland, MO 63459

Dear Ms. Huston,

I apologize for the delay in sending this recommendation. For more than two decades I have maintained an orderly record-keeping system regarding each and every one of my students, but I apparently misfiled the information on Shayla Newcome and had to get out the dowsing rod to find her. In response to your query: Ms. Newcome was my student six years ago. Having located the appropriate slim green record book in the lower left drawer of my desk, I note that she received a B in my Intermediate Fiction Writing class, having completed, if I am deciphering my own handwritten notes correctly, a short story intended to be a fictionalization of the pope's childhood. Whether this indicates that Ms. Newcome is or is not to be entrusted with the precious lives of small children, I have no idea. At least she did not—as many of my undergraduates seem to enjoy doing—submit a vivid and celebratory depiction of murder and mayhem, complete with flesh-eating robots, werewolves, resurrections from the crypt, or some combination of the above. Students' lives have been cheapened in ways of which they remain blissfully clueless, because of so much TV.

The only other information I can offer you about Ms. Newcome is that during the semester she was enrolled in my class she was having a difficult time. Students don't generally confide in me regarding their personal crises (I am not known for being particularly approachable or cuddly), but Ms. Newcome did, and I remember that in the interstices of our conversation she chewed at the lime-green polish—an unfortunate color—on her fingernails. A few weeks later I asked if her situation had improved and she said it had not, but she was "learning to accommodate." I found that impressive, and remembering Ms. Newcome now—though my file drawer contains thousands of lives[*] for which I often find myself feeling accountable—I realize I am well disposed in her favor; in fact, I thoroughly urge you to offer her a job.

Why? Because, as a student of literature and creative writing, Ms. Newcome honed crucial traits that will be of use to you: imagination, patience, resourcefulness, and empathy. The reading and writing of fiction both requires and instills empathy—the insertion of oneself into the life of another.

[*] By recent estimate I have penned more than 1,300 letters of recommendation, many of them enthusiastic, some a cry of despair.

I believe Ms. Newcome eminently capable of the work for which she has applied.

With good wishes for your tiny charges,
Jay Fitger, Professor of Creative Writing and English
Payne University

Dear Associate Vice Provost Millhouse,

The purpose of this letter is to bolster the promotion and tenure case of Professor Martina Ali here at our esteemed institution of higher learning. I am not a member of Professor Ali's Film Studies Program, but the Honorable Pooh-Bahs in your office have decreed that P&T dossiers be encumbered with no fewer than six missives of support, and Professor Ali is one of only three faculty members in her own modest department. Such is the wisdom that prevails at Payne.

I'll get around to my evaluation of Professor Ali. But I have a few other things on my mind also, and it would be foolish of me, I think—it would be remiss—if I didn't take this opportunity to address a few of them. After all, how often does a lowly professor of creative writing and English have the ear of the associate VP? Perhaps I should intercalate my own laundry list of items throughout my evaluation of Martina—she does stellar research—threading them into the fabric of this letter like stinging nettles. We'll see how things go.

First—Professor Ali's monograph on warfare in European film: While some members of her discipline have adopted an almost psychedelic approach to their choice of material, delivering conference papers and fashioning entire semester-long courses on the topic of toothpaste commercials or videos of tumbleweeds bounding along by the side of a road,[*] Professor Ali is invested in significance. Her work combines rigorous historical research, film scholarship, and psychoanalytic theory—and her goal is enlightenment, not obfuscation. She has justifiably won the Longfreth Prize (twice!), the panel of judges likening her scholarship to the work of Alperovitz and Harms, pioneers in the field.

Ali is publishing in some of her discipline's top venues. *Comparative Film and Culture* in particular—a highly selective, peer-reviewed journal—is a scholarly coup.

Given her publications, her increasingly national reputation, and her teaching record (eleven advisees!), Ali is a shoo-in. We both know that. I hope her department chair musters the reams of paperwork needed to satisfy your army of bean counters in Lefferts Hall. A divagation here: Have you entered Willard Hall lately? In case, over there among the functional radiators and other amenities in Lefferts, you've forgotten that English faculty members are living in a construction zone, allow me to

[*] See Professor Jorg Masterson's infamous class, Dis/guise and Dis/gust, to which students are invited to bring "rancid food and a costume or mask."

give you a virtual tour. The front and back doors of our building are blocked—sealed and crisscrossed with yellow tape as if to indicate a crime scene—so you must enter through the basement. But don't use the elevator, a nightmarish herk-and-jerk contraption known to hijack its occupants and leave them stranded midfloor. You can't access the second (Econ) floor in any case: a silken banner advises you to PARDON OUR MESS!—a euphemistic reference to the fact that workers equipped with respirators are spilling toxins onto our heads in the servants' quarters, where, once you overlook the chipped and ancient linoleum and the cracks in the wallboard, you will find a sign that welcomes visitors, eloquently, to the Department of ENGLI_H.

Professor Ali's teaching record is, without doubt, superb. The only smudge on it results from the fact that some clueless sadist assigned her an introductory lecture course during her first two semesters on campus (which would have been an occasion for spectacular failure for most junior faculty—but Professor Ali's evaluations were well above par).

A note here—excuse the indelicacy—on the men's room in Willard: a subtle but incessant dripping from a pipe in the ceiling (perhaps from the Jacuzzi or bidet being installed for our Economics colleagues) is gradually transforming this previously charming depot into a fetid cavern. The tile floor is often slick with liquids and, because desperate citizens have propped the door open, odors now regularly waft out into the hall. I might as well set my desk next to the urinals.

42

In sum, Ali's is an open-and-shut case, yet another occasion for faculty members to set their work aside in order to cobble together encomiums and tributes like train cars chugging in an endless loop through campus. If faculty were able—even encouraged—to dedicate the same amount of time to our research and writing, we might stop sinking like a stone in the national rankings and have a chance to be a reasonably respectable school.

Finally, as for your recent memo on financial prudence: Good lord, man. We know about the funding crunch, we aren't idiots; but we also know that your fiscal fix is being applied selectively. For those in the sciences and social sciences, sacrifice will come in the form of fewer varieties of pâté on the lunch trays. For English: seven defections/retirements in three years and not one replaced; two graduate programs no longer permitted to accept new students; and a Captain Queeg–like sociologist at the helm. The junior faculty in our department will surely abandon their posts at the first opportunity, while the elder statesmen—I speak here for myself—may exact a more punishing revenge by refusing to retire.

I thoroughly endorse Professor Martina Ali's bid for promotion to associate professor with tenure.

Cordially and with the usual succinctness,
Jay Fitger

Good Afternoon, Committee Members—with cc to Eleanor
Acton, Director:

This is the third letter I have written on behalf of Mr. Darren
Browles, who recently received from your office a computerized notice that, of his three required letters of recommendation, only two have been received. Why each application to
Bentham necessitates *three written* LORs I leave to sages and
philosophers to decipher. As for the letters in Mr. Browles's case
(your office has refused to identify their authors): let's count
them. **One** is mine, dated September 3 (with a follow-up/coda
on October 5). **Two** is the letter from his foreign language advisor; I just wandered across the quad and spoke to Herr Zim-
munt to secure his *jawohl* in regard to this endorsement. **Letter
Three**, Browles informs me, was originally to have come from
Helena Stang, who led him on an e-mail goose chase for over a
month until finally reporting, as if from her satin fainting couch,
that she was "too busy." He had no choice at that point but
to turn to his administrative advisor, Martin Glenk, who (unbeknownst to poor Browles) wrests fleeting moments of joy from
the opportunity to denigrate my students.

Armed with these bitter herbs of information, I undertook this morning the short but unhappy stroll past the men's room (the toilets of which send their constant flushing sound through the vent in my office) to the literature wing of our department. Typically I am loath to poke about in that arm of the building, around the corner from the WELCOME TO ENGLI_H sign and the faded sofas on which, after hours, the undergraduates presumably enjoy one another's favors. To be blunt: many of the literature faculty and I are no longer speaking, and a third of their number, due to a construction project in our hallowed hall, have moved their offices to remote outposts of campus, delighting in the knowledge that their colleagues will be unable to find them. Logically, one might suggest that I solicit the assistance of my department chair, but he is a professor of sociology, appointed by the university's warlords to rule our asylum until the inmates exhibit greater pliability and calm.

In any event, I did ultimately locate the elusive Glenk, who, after wiping his nose on the back of his sleeve, refused to confirm or deny the existence of his LOR on Browles's behalf. In case he sends or has sent a letter, allow me to provide some context for it: Glenk is a merciless and vengeful chucklehead—an Eliot scholar suffering from the delusion that he is a poet, though he hasn't written a word of any significance for a dozen years.

Eleanor, I appeal to you: Darren Browles doesn't need three LORs, and his *Bartleby* novel needn't be subject to the sordid aspersions of a cretin like Glenk. Don't let him be punished for my lack of popularity among my colleagues, present or past. (I include the word "past" to encompass any rivalry or unpleasantness between the two of us during the Seminar; our personal discord has no bearing on Browles, and I'd like to spare him the politicized trauma of our earlier years.)

Seeking to bury the hatchet or at least dull its blade,
Jay

P.S. (to Eleanor): Speaking of our Seminar years, I got a letter from Troy Larpenteur last week—resurfaced at last, somewhere in Ohio. His tone was cautiously upbeat, but I suspect he has been unwell for a very long time. He needs a recommendation, of course. Do you know if he's been in touch with anyone else? Would Madelyne TV have kept track of him?

November 16, 2009
ITech Solutions
271 Riverview Way
Dubuque, Iowa 52003
Attention: Maxine Wells

Dear Ms. Wells,

I am overjoyed by the opportunity to recommend Mr. Duffy Napp to your firm. Mr. Napp currently serves as the sole remaining member of what used to be the "Tech Help team" in our Department of English, and he clearly suffers under the burden of our collective ignorance. Mr. Napp demonstrates all the winsome ebullience one expects these days from a young person more inclined to socialize with machines rather than human beings. His approach to problem solving is characterized by sullenness punctuated by occasional brief bouts of good judgment.

Whatever I can do to assist in your—or any other firm's—hiring of Mr. Napp I will accomplish with resolution and zeal.

Hopefully, and with fingers crossed,
Jason T. Fitger
Professor of Creative Writing and English

November 20, 2009
Gar Canfield
Zentex Corporation
8591 Taylor Boulevard
Panama, Ohio 45807

Dear Mr. Canfield,

This letter very warmly endorses the application of Troy Larpenteur, who has informed me of his desire to secure a position as sales associate in the Zentex Corporation.

I have known Troy Larpenteur for twenty-three years: we attended graduate school together. Troy was widely acknowledged to be one of the most gifted and original writers to pass through the infamous Seminar under the tutelage of H. Reginald Hanf. (If you don't know Hanf's work: please head straight to the library or bookstore—I give you leave to put this letter aside and come back to it later—to find a copy of *Testimony in Red,* a finalist for the National Book Award, which, in the absence of cronyism among the judges that year, would have won.)

Though he appears not to have mentioned it on his résumé, Troy Larpenteur published a brilliant lyrical novella called *Second Mind,* which was showered with praise but underappreciated, as are many pathbreaking works; it is now out of print. Subsequently he labored for the better part of a decade on his magnum opus, a novel, which was lost along with his pregnant wife when the cabin lent to them by a friend, a cabin in which they were taking a long-awaited vacation, was struck by lightning during a storm. The randomness of his wife Navia's death—the vacation had been urged upon them; Troy had driven to the store for supplies before the storm's scheduled arrival; the car got a flat tire and Troy stumbled back down the flooded road to find the cabin in flames—defeated his belief in art and quelled his aspirations. He never returned to the novel. He moved to India, where Navia had spent her early childhood, and wiped himself off the grid for a dozen years.

You may be searching this letter for references to Troy's "relevant experience." (Troy asked me to limit myself in this recommendation to the qualities and attributes that will make him an asset to your firm.) Let me suggest that, no matter the variety of employment, there is nothing more relevant or crucial than an aptitude for original thought and imaginative expression. When I think back twenty-three years to the sight of Troy across from me at the Seminar table, his hair looking as if he had slept on the floor of the library by the vending machines (he usually had), his face alight with intelligence and anticipation, I believe the best years of my life will be the ones in which I had the privilege of hearing him read his work aloud to our group. Even HRH—Professor Hanf—fell silent when Troy slid his pages from the battered portmanteau in which he liked to keep his writing; we waited on tenterhooks, knowing that whatever Troy read would alter something within us, changing the way in which we understood language and its cumulative power, the way it made our lives feel capacious, infusing us each week during our three- or four-hour-long sessions with the sensation that we were at long last about to apprehend . . . what? Unlike many of his peers, myself included, Troy was free of egoism. He cared about his work, and others' work, as opposed to "success." He was, and remains, an intellectually nimble, brilliant, generous man.

I understand that Troy has applied for the position of sales associate. This is a foreign concept to me: here in the academy we are unaccustomed to salesmanship of any kind, even to the faintest of efforts to make ourselves presentable or attractive to others. Nevertheless I can readily attest to Troy Larpenteur's seriousness, his quick intelligence, and his kindness. He is not gregarious—I do not envision him cracking jokes by the water cooler—but he is a man of great integrity and depth.

Forgive the meanderings in what should have been a more businesslike letter. (Blaise Pascal: *I apologize that my letter is so long; I lacked the time to make it shorter.*) I have written more than 1,300 letters of recommendation (I keep precise records), and were it possible I would assemble the many laudatory phrases from this bloated collection and apply them like a poultice to Troy Larpenteur's pain.

Of course I have failed to do here what he asked of me: I seldom lived up to his example. For reasons I won't bother to go into now, Troy might once have harbored an unfavorable opinion of me, but he is too generous. I will be forever in his debt.

Please hire this exceptional man, whose many fine qualities must surely find an appreciative home in your corporation.

Sincerely,
Jason T. Fitger
Professor of Creative Writing and English
Author, *Stain; Alphabetical Stars; Save Me for Later;* and *Transfer of Affection*

Dear Carole—and Relevant Committee Members,

Pa Vang has requested that I support her application to Payne's Students of Distinction Fellowship Fund. A cursory glance at her transcript, with its tidy, monotonous fishing line of A's, should suffice to recommend her. All I have to add is that she is as bright in person as she is on paper; she has not accumulated her perfect scores by fraudulent or suspicious means; and she appears to be a pleasant human being. (I am of the opinion that pleasantness is immaterial, but I am aware of brilliant but "difficult" students who have been denied funds.)

Ms. Vang is not difficult. She is ambitious and diligent, a sophomore literature major with—may god offer her succor—a desire to become a professor of Engli_h.

The VP's hectoring campaign about our paucity of resources continues, but you and I know that for students like Vang, the money is out there. Tell Sidney to open his purse strings and cough up the funds.

Carole: I'm still hoping you'll agree to have lunch with me—nothing formal or off-campus if you aren't comfortable yet with the idea. But maybe I could swing by your office with that artichoke salad you used to favor?

JTF

P.S.: I heard about the altercation at the diversity committee meeting, and I understand that my name was invoked. Didn't I warn you about sitting near Janet? Did she take you on her favorite fault-finding tour through *Transfer of Affection*?

Confidential Reference for WJRX17794 Cynthia Goldberg
Please complete the following to the best of your knowledge:

1. How long and in what capacity have you known the applicant?

Greetings, committee members. I have known Ms. Goldberg for almost three years. She was my student in two undergraduate classes: the twentieth-century American survey, which begins with

2. Give a brief description of the applicant's aptitude and/or past performance.

Ms. Goldberg received a B+ in the chaotic welter of the survey, an introductory course designed by the university to function as part academic lecture, part flash mob, because of the unrestricted and steadily rising numbers of enrolled students, 10 percent of whom failed due to ennui or inebriation (the class met at 8:00 a.m.) and subsequently faded back into the larger undifferentiated ooze of the campus. In the short story class she received a B-, perhaps unfairly. The size of the group

3. Do you know of any reasons why the applicant should not be given responsibility as stated on the list of qualifications above?

First, I'll finish my response to question #2—your blasted form cut me off. The survey class enrolled seventy-five undergraduates, many of whom signed up because of my reputation for Sturm und Drang; bored by the material—that is, *books*—they nonetheless enjoy watching me pull at what remains of my hair while I stamp back and forth in paroxysms of incredulity caused by the half-baked ideas casually lobbed in my direction from the back of the room. Not granted a teaching assistant to help with the evaluation of essays, I was forced to require in-class exams rather than allow the students to draft and revise their work in the quiet sanctity of their dorm rooms. In an ideal world, I would outlaw literature exams entirely; I would also eschew the twin barbarities of "attendance" and "participation" as grading criteria, necessitated by workload increase. Ms. Goldberg

4. Are there any other comments you would like to add?

Yes: I would like to finish my fucking sentences. I suppose your organization is to be commended for not resorting to the absurd array of little black boxes in which recommenders like me are asked to rate applicants according to [ ] likelihood of earning a Nobel Prize, [ ] personal hygiene, [ ] ability to form coherent sentences not randomly punctuated by "like" or "really" or other verbal fluff, but given that your damnable form has cut me off every time I initiate a

5. Thank you!

November 25, 2009
Neologisms Conference Committee
Denwood University
42A Roosevelt Hall
Denwood, NC 28078
Attention: Harold Duvlavsky

Dear Harold:

Ms. Rowena Handel has recently submitted a proposal to your Neologisms Conference—a proposal, she now belatedly understands, that was to be accompanied by a letter of reference.

Ms. Handel is neither my advisee nor my student: she pinned me down outside the men's room—conveniently adjacent to my office, so that my writing and research are invariably conducted to the flushing of waste—and, with the anxious desperation for which PhD candidates are justifiably known, trailed behind me into my office, installed herself in the red vinyl chair that has cradled the backsides of thousands, and insisted I listen to a frantic rendition of her proposal for the purposes of writing, on her behalf, this exalted document.

It is 2:00 p.m., tomorrow is Thanksgiving, and here in my office the snow is accreting in small picturesque clumps against the ill-fitting window, which rattles in its Dickensian case-

56

ment. The other faculty, including Ms. Handel's advisors, have retreated like whack-a-moles into obscure campus locales or left town on vacation. Divorced, somewhat recently spurned, and therefore doomed to spend the holiday with two vegetarians from the Classics Department, I was apparently the only living member of the faculty the unfortunate Ms. Handel was able to find. That said: her proposal—entirely outside my field—appears to have merit. In particular, her examination of inventive phrases related to issues of gender identity—though of no interest to me—is probably worth sharing with a collegiate audience.

Note: My magnanimity and spirit of service will not extend so far as to persuade me to submit to your online recommendation, despite Ms. Handel's willingness to enlighten me as to its mysteries or to prostrate herself on my linoleum floor. True, her proposal's endorsement will be delayed until next week, but Thanksgiving—though tainted with oppression and bloodshed—is a national holiday, and your request for an LOR specifies only a date of *submission,* not receipt. Therefore by 3:20 p.m. this letter will be deposited in the quaint rectangular mouth of the blue mailbox, now quite sparkling and emphatic in the new-fallen snow; and I presume you will note the date of its postmark. Ms. Handel clawed repeatedly at her arms when I mentioned the mailbox (she asked if I had considered using the Pony Express), but, in the absence of an alternative mutually agreed-upon plan, she acquiesced.

Wishing you a scintillating conference,
Jay Fitger, Professor, Recommender-for-Hire
Payne University

P.S.: Harold—I saw your name on the list of Bentham advisory board members. While I don't doubt your qualifications or your caliber as a scholar, I was under the impression that Bentham advisors (and obviously residents) were to be literary artists rather than academicians. Has that policy changed? Eleanor Acton—the new director—and I are long-ago classmates and onetime friends, and I've sent her several recommendations on behalf of a student novelist, Darren Browles, but have received no positive reply. Now I'm wondering if Eleanor's years in the corporate world have warped her—and if any promising writer I might recommend to Bentham will, in favor of scholars regurgitating rancid tidbits of Derrida or Cixous, be turned away. Would you put in a good word for Browles? And: any insight—confidential of course—that you could provide on a possible seismic shift in Bentham's raison d'être would be most appreciated.

December 2, 2009
Catfish Catering
790 South Campus Boulevard
Rana Abdul, General Manager

Dear Ms. Abdul,

Seth Padoman has asked that I serve as a reference vis-à-vis his bid to secure an entry-level job in your catering establishment.

Let me be candid: the job market for young employment seekers is abysmal; otherwise, Mr. Padoman, who graduated with a BA in English last spring, would set his sights considerably higher. When last I spoke with him he was sheepishly dejected and confessed to living on microwaved food in his sister's basement; I advised him to man up, polish his résumé, marshal his references (including mine), and retain an optimistic façade.

Still. Catfish Catering—all too familiar to those of us immured in the culinary universe of inexpensive university-sanctioned cuisine—is one of the most gruesome sources of provender on the planet. Oil (god only knows whether you're using K-Y Jelly, lard, or some less well recognized lubricant) appears to be your primary ingredient regardless of the category of food. Last year at the banquet honoring the installation of our new provost, I made the mistake (yes, it was my error, I admit it) of consuming a modest portion of tilapia from the groaning board; I was ill for three days. Substances I would never knowingly introduce to my body had apparently proliferated within it and were then rapidly expelled in unspeakable gouts. I counted myself fortunate, at the end of a week of gastrointestinal crisis, to be able to walk.

Seth Padoman is a bright-eyed, well-intentioned young man: not the most accomplished among recent clusters (in class he was perhaps best known as the author of a sci-fi tale about a mutant clan of gun-wielding arachnids that assumed control of a cocaine factory in Mexico), but eager and ambitious. He deserves a future, and therefore I recommend him to you on the condition that you not allow him to consume any foodstuffs produced by your place of business.

Yours in digestive health,
J. T. Fitger
Professor, Department of English

Carole:

Let this humble communiqué serve as my recommendation for Lee Rosenthal: the poor kid tells me he has applied for a spring semester job in your office. He can read and write; he's not unsightly; and he doesn't appear to be addicted to illegal substances prior to 3:00 p.m. Set him to work typing something. He finished the first half of my Junior/Senior Creative Writing Workshop with a B+ and is currently laboring away on a final short story—prescient soul—about a college graduate who lands a meaningless entry-level position in his father's law firm, compromising his iconoclastic ideals and ambitions to make some cold hard cash.

Which reminds me: I heard what I sincerely hope was a scurrilous rumor to the effect that you are searching for work outside the velvet bonds of our institution. Be honest with me: Did Janet say something truly objectionable at the diversity committee meeting? (At an all-campus congress just before we divorced, she actually read aloud from *Transfer of Affection*, as if the novel itself were some sort of indictment. I admit to weaving with the threads of real life on my loom, in *Transfer* and especially in *Stain;*[*] but the fictional, philandering George Fitzgerald in those books isn't me [I only cheated on Janet once], and the fictional Nella, despite her rapaciousness, is not my ex-wife.)

To the point: Carole—it would be shortsighted and foolish for you to leave campus on my account. From this day forward, I won't call your office more than once a week, and I promise never again to stop by unannounced with your favorite artichoke salad—which I ended up eating alone, by the way, on a cold metal bench on the quad, attracting the attention of itinerant polemicists and pamphleteers.

I will leave you in peace. And of course if I can't persuade you to stay, I'd be willing to write you a recommendation . . .

Deep breath and new subject. Interview Rosenthal. Just ask him to keep his left arm covered, unless you want to be exposed to a fleshy panoply of R-rated tattoos.

With the usual professionalism and longing,
JF

* The *Times* called it "an insider's seedy, salacious guide to the notorious Seminar"—which probably nudged the book toward a second printing.

Dear Ted:

Via this LOR I hereby nominate Gwendolyn Hoch-Dunn for this semester's English Undergraduate Thesis Award. Ms. Hoch-Dunn has a 3.9 GPA and is currently completing, under my supervision, a thirty-five-page monograph on Edith Wharton's *The House of Mirth:* specifically, an examination of romantic and economic trajectories in the novel. Hoch-Dunn is a superb student: she will graduate magna cum laude in spring, spend a year enlarging her personal horizon by teaching English abroad, and then succeed at whatever she chooses.

Perhaps you've familiarized yourself by now with the faculty's areas of concentration and are wondering why Ms. Hoch-Dunn is laboring away on this particular project under my direction rather than Albert Tyne's, given that Tyne is a Wharton special-ist. The fact is that Tyne, never appealing in person, has become a lecherous eyesore avoided as a matter of course by all female (and most male) students, one of whom informed me back in September—you may want to check in on this, Ted, at your earliest convenience—that instead of visiting the urinals in the men's room Tyne has been pissing into old wine bottles, then

63

(thank god for small favors) replacing the corks and arranging his collection in a foul gold ring around the perimeter of his office. I don't doubt the truth of this accusation: I haven't seen Tyne in the men's room for years. Not being paid an administrator's exalted salary, I have no intention of violating the sanctum of his uriniferous lair in order to do anything corrective, and it occurs to me that this particular duty might appropriately fall to a sociologist . . .

Poor Ms. Hoch-Dunn. Her other advisory options, subtracting those who have entered phased retirement or sabbatical, those who always refuse student requests for assistance as a matter of course, and the clinically insane, were Donna Lovejoy (now circulating her CV like a blackjack dealer at every conference in order to extricate herself from our department), Sandra Atherman (as am I, she is laden like a burro with advisees every semester), and me. Lance West advises the rhetoricians (and having, inexplicably, been turned down for the Campiello Award, he will probably be gone by the end of this year). Technically, yes, Ms. Hoch-Dunn might have queried Zander Hesseldine, but he is currently interested only in postcolonial theory, whereas I am—the students understand this—not afraid or ashamed to be a dinosaur, a person who reads and teaches novels (not "texts"), and who instills whenever possible during class sessions a fast-fading (and, to the students, possibly retrograde or endearing) humanistic agenda, emphasizing literary inquiry into the human experience and the human condition. As far as period and subject matter, my tastes are eclectic, but

I remain generally unmoved by floating houses and mythical grandmothers returned from the dead, which are—let's be honest here—the contemporary equivalent of elves and unicorns.

Ms. Hoch-Dunn is, I believe, one of the best undergraduate students we have been fortunate enough to count among our majors in recent years. She is a bright spot amid the intellectual and moral decay of our department, a decay now physically manifested in our surroundings (the fax machine is broken again; a large chunk of the ceiling fell and crushed it while Gunnar was attempting to use it this morning) at the behest of the dean, the associate vice provost, and their brutal band of incompetent henchmen.

Give the award to Hoch-Dunn, and God save us all.

In dire camaraderie,
Jay

P.S.: I'm sure you read the campus newspaper's article about our venerable colleagues in the Economics Department? Not only do their salaries make ours look like an eleven-year-old's allowance; they will now be able to offer funding to every student admitted to the econ major. An idea here, Ted: Why don't you inquire in the dean's office if—once they close our department down for good—we might be rehired to clean, perhaps with cotton swabs dipped in olive oil, the gold leaf surely to be installed in the brand-new fiefdom on the Econ floor?

December 15, 2009
Torreforde State University MFA Program
Admissions
77 Welshire Hall
Torreforde, MI 49004

Dear Readers and Committee Members,

Iris Temple has applied to your MFA program in fiction and has asked me to support, via this LOR, her application. I find this difficult to do, not because Ms. Temple is unqualified (she is a gifted and disciplined writer and has published several stories in appropriately obscure venues), but because your program at Torreforde State offers its graduate writers no funding or aid of any kind—an unconscionable act of piracy and a grotesque, systemic abuse of vulnerable students, to whom you extend the false hope that writing a $50,000 check to your institution will be the first step toward artistic success.

Do not suppose that I object to writing programs in general (I myself am a proud graduate of the Seminar) or that I indulge in the all-too-tiresome hand-wringing about the proliferation of MFA programs and the pseudo crisis of "too many writers." If every member of the human race evinced a fondness for literature and even a moderate level of dexterity with the written word, I would be a happier, if not more well-adjusted, man. The

66

trouble arrives when students are led to expect tenure-track jobs (those days are behind us) or champagne and caviar parties at Farrar, Straus and Giroux. They might as well invest in Powerball tickets: book sales continue their downward spiral, and the launch of a first or a subsequent volume is rarely the occasion for the unbridled hoopla that, in earlier days, it once was.

A quick outline of my own publication history will perhaps be instructive.

My first novel, *Stain*, sold twice as many copies as did my other three books combined, either because the marketplace, twenty years ago, was still romantically invested in the idea of a debut author, or because no one else had written an R-rated (if fictionalized) tell-all about H. Reginald Hanf and the Seminar. My literary doppelgänger, George Fitzgerald, was zealously reviled, and the novel feted, and I assumed that my success had just begun.

Alphabetical Stars and *Save Me for Later* manifested my attempts to "stretch myself" and to demonstrate my range as a writer: I didn't want to be typecast as a gossipy satirist limited to the material in his own backyard. But what did I know about cold war defectors and their families, or about NASA in the 1960s? Not enough: the *Chicago Tribune* called *Save Me for Later* a "poor choice of subject, a sort of weird homage to the

Stasi," and *The Boston Globe* claimed that *Alphabetical Stars* portrayed John Glenn as "emotionally deformed."

So. I returned in *Transfer of Affection* to familiar ground—to *Stain's* handsome protagonist, George Fitzgerald, and to the petty rivalries and comic (and sexual) misalliances in an academic milieu. Most readers think *Stain* is my best book, but *Transfer* is more sophisticated, more nuanced, smarter. Even so, it failed to move off the shelves. It also hastened the demise of my marriage, poor George Fitzgerald's romantic blunders hinting too clearly at a few of my own. As for current and future projects, I have been working somewhat halfheartedly on a new novel, the early chapters of which my agent greeted with all the enthusiasm of a farmer presented with a bucket of dung.

The point of this little digression, in regard to Ms. Temple, is not to discourage the practice of writing: What, after all, is a writer's life without a dose of despair? The point is that literary endeavor has always been riddled with frustration but in recent years has become increasingly formidable; ergo my revulsion for programs like yours that, under the false pretense of support, function as succubi draining the bank accounts and lifeblood of unsuspecting students like Iris Temple, whom I (warmly) recommend to you only on the condition that you offer her free tuition, at a minimum, as well as a frank disclosure regarding

a. the job market encountered by your recent graduates;

b. the dismal state of publishing;

c. declining literacy rates and plummeting support for the arts.

Should Ms. Temple matriculate at Torreforde State under these conditions, I shall wish her well and be the first to welcome her to "the writing life," which, despite its horrors, is possibly one of the few sorts of lives worth living at all.

Collegially,
Jay Fitger
Professor, Creative Writing and English—Payne

Honorable Internship Coordinator:

This letter's purpose is to recommend to you—in the capacity of unpaid labor, presumably licking envelopes and knocking on doors—Malinda Heisman, a student in my Multicultural American Literature class. Malinda is an A student, a wide-eyed earnest individual who will undoubtedly benefit from a few months spent among the self-serving pontificates in the senator's office.

Malinda is intelligent; she is organized; she is well spoken. Given her aptitude for research (unlike most undergraduates, she has moved beyond Wikipedia), I am sure that she will soon learn that the senator, his leathern face permanently embossed with a gruesome rictus of feigned cheer, has consistently voted against funds for higher education and has cosponsored multiple narrow-minded backwater proposals that will make it ever more difficult for her to repay the roughly $38,000 in debt that the average graduate of our institution inherits—along with a lovely blue tassel—on the day of commencement.

Malinda's final essay in my class—here it is on my desk, among a cast of thousands—is a windy but assiduous reading of Jamaica Kincaid's *At the Bottom of the River*. The essay demonstrates strong writing skills and rigorous thinking. Allow Malinda the privilege of laboring in your office for nothing (she'll probably continue to work nights as a barista in the coffee empire), and I am confident you will be making, though perhaps not in the ways you might have intended, a remarkable contribution to her education.

With all best wishes, I remain
Your devoted public servant,
Jay Fitger, Professor of the Lost Arts
Payne University

Dear Elegant Madelyne, aka MTV:

It's been too long—ten years?—since we ran into each other at the Western Writers conference in Denver. I remember sitting with you at the hotel bar, each of us (all right, yes, full disclosure, it was mainly me) unpacking the sordid facts of our professional and then our personal lives. Janet and I were still together then, but not very happily, and you had just gotten married, and you had come to the conference for a panel on writing about trauma and disability because you were interviewing for the job at Caxton, in the High Plains of Wyoming. I take my hat off to you, truly. I hope you've forgotten most of what you learned, that weekend, about me.

You may already have guessed that I'm writing to ask you a favor. I know that Caxton is designated for PTSD sufferers and survivors of military violence (I remember you telling me about the phantom pain in your husband's leg and the way he used to wake at night, convinced his foot had returned, his missing toes scrabbling against the sheet), but my understanding is that you occasionally treat civilian PTSD as well. And so I'm wondering if, out there on the plains, perhaps midwinter or spring, you might find yourself with a vacancy and be inspired, for the sake of that evening at the conference or in memory of our Seminar days, to accept as a working client an exceptional student and advisee, Darren Browles. I wouldn't bother to plead his case with you under ordinary conditions—that goes without saying. Of course he's working on an unprecedented novel (I'm including the opening chapter here so you can see for yourself)—but more germane in this case, he's in dire need and probably meets 90 percent of the criteria for a posttraumatic classification. May I explain?

First, he has endured the intellectual abuse and collective lunacy for which the university system is widely known; **second,** due to administrative snafus and an Orwellian effort to quash graduate programs in literature and the arts, his funding has been rescinded; and **third,** I wrote him a recommendation to Bentham, and not only did Eleanor deny him (you heard, I'm sure, that she's director now), she slammed his project. Browles wouldn't show me the text of her refusal, but he shuffled grimly into my office with the news that Eleanor herself had turned him down, setting aside time in her busy schedule to communicate at length her belief that the entire concept of his novel was "derivative." *That's the whole point:* Browles's book, *Accountant in a Bordello* (it's a working title), is an ironic homage to *Bartleby.* Browles stood by my desk, immobile, and stared down at his shoes; I could see that he'd almost persuaded

73

himself of Eleanor's malignant opinions,[*] and I wanted to leap out of my chair and shake him and say, "It's not you she wants to annihilate, you poor clueless idiot; it's me." This is vicarious decades-delayed payback. We were all in HRH's Seminar for the same reason: to compete for Reg's roving capricious interest, to gain his hard-won attention—because he was known for making the careers of young writers, for discovering even in the roughest of efforts some glimmering ingot. And even if it was generally understood that his few designees might be credulous emperors modeling new clothes, that didn't matter, because his brother was an editor in New York.

Eleanor is still bitter that Reg was behind me. She is still bitter about the publication of *Stain*.

Two decades later, let me tell you the truth, TV, a few simple facts:

1. I would have done *anything*—I would have sold my own mother into slavery—in order to publish that first book, and HRH was my connection to the publishing world.

2. Of course I took his advice and "spiced up" the narrative; what else could I do? But I *did* cut the scene in which George and Esther tear up the pages of their professor's novel and make

---

[*] I should have warned him that Eleanor played Lady Macbeth in college.

love in the tumble of his words. One night when I was working on the edits, Troy showed up at my apartment with a bottle of Wild Turkey and spent five or six hours politely insisting that, as the honorable person he knew me to be, I was going to let that bit go—a considerable sacrifice that didn't lessen Eleanor's rage.

3. Eleanor goaded and disliked me even before she slept with me. She used to call me Jay the Obtuse,[*] and when Reg noticed the animosity between us he began subtly to urge me to see her as the prototype for George Fitzgerald's libidinous antagonist, Esther, in *Stain*.

Enough. Moving on. Here's what I'm asking, TV: let Browles unwind at Caxton for a month or two, longer if that's feasible on your end. Offer him solitude, and let him be shielded from the shit and the failures to come. I vouch for him completely (alter ego, you ask?), and I promise he won't set off firecrackers under a fellow resident's cabin. You could probably include him in some of the therapeutic sessions; I'm sure he'd benefit, as would anyone—myself included, god knows.

Apologies for the rant and the nostalgic detour. Like Scrooge, less than a week before the clamor of Christmas, I'm making

[*] NB: Because of my obsession with *Jude the Obscure*, Janet still calls me "Jay the Obtuse" now and then, but it doesn't sound as cruel when she says it.

this last-minute request with every scrap of human warmth I've got left to muster. I'm the tide propelling a shipwrecked man to your doorstep. Please take Browles on. I guarantee he'd be amenable to periodic tasks around the compound—groundskeeping and whatnot—if that would be useful.

With admiration, and wishing you a peaceful holiday, I remain Your friend,
Jay

P.S.: Have you heard from Troy? He's stateside again, and I know he always had a soft spot for you—I'm bewildered and a bit chagrined that he's reached out to *me* . . .

January 4, 2010
Kathleen Quam
Associate Chair, Comp/Rhetoric
Lattimore Community College
16 Fountain Place
Lattimore, IL 60491

Dear Professor Quam,

Alex Ruefle has prevailed upon me to support his teaching application to your department, which I gather is hiring adjunct faculty members exclusively, bypassing the tenure track with its attendant health benefits, job security, and salaries on which a human being might reasonably live. Perhaps your institution should cut to the chase and put its entire curriculum online, thereby sparing Ruefle the need to move to Lattimore, wherever that is. You could prop him up in a broom closet in his apartment, poke him with the butt end of a mop when you need him to cough up a lecture on Caribbean fiction or the passive voice, and then charge your students a thousand dollars each to correct the essays their classmates have downloaded from a website. Such is the future of education.

How do I know Alex? During the early years of his doctoral studies in English at Payne, he was assigned to me as an RA; this was back in the precrisis era, a dulcet time in our university's history when faculty were allotted luxuries such as research support, access to a working copy machine, and paper and pen. (Currently, we count ourselves fortunate to have functional toilets. I don't know what your living conditions are at Lattimore—tidy and sterile, I suspect—but here, given a construction project initiated on behalf of our Economics faculty, who Must Be Kept Comfortable at All Times, we are alternately frozen and nearly smoked, via pestilent fumes, out of our building. Between the construction dust and the radiators emitting erratic bursts of steam heat, the intrepid faculty members who have remained in their offices over the winter break are humid with sweat and dusted with ash and resemble two-legged cutlets dredged in flour.)

In any case, Alex. I leave to others the task of evaluating his thesis[*] and will limit myself to discussing his performance as my RA, which was more than adequate. Ruefle is highly capable, efficient, and independent. I confess that some of the assignments I gave him might have been easy to misinterpret, based as they were on episodes of my own life and experience. (At that time I still indulged in sweet dreams of success, blissfully ignorant of the relentless downward drift of my career, my

---

[*] I assume he listed me as a reference because of the retirement and demise, respectively, of his two thesis advisors: it took Ruefle fourteen years to earn the doctorate. During that time he became a fixture here at Payne, beginning his studies as a vigorous man and, after marrying and acquiring multiple children, staggering across the PhD finish line in late middle age.

novel-in-progress, when published, to be greeted by a sphinx-like silence in the press, the wrath of my [now] ex-wife, and the near universal condemnation, on campus, from readers who failed to understand the concept of satire.) But Ruefle seldom lifted an eyebrow. Like a waiter committing a lengthy order to memory, he would listen and nod, hands in his pockets, and then disappear, presumably heading home to work by himself, in his footie pajamas, uninterrupted by the demands or neuroses of his supervisor. He always got the work done.

I urge you to hire Alex Ruefle and to offer him a position commensurate with his multiple decades of education and his abilities—that is, a position well above, both in salary and rank, the one your college has posted.

Hoping the New Year inspires conscientious behavior in one and all, I remain
Jason Fitger, Professor of Creative Writing and English
Payne University

Dear C. R. Young,

Ms. Tara Tappani knocked at my office door this morning and, with the air of a woman wearing diamonds and furs, entered the icy enclosure in which I work, perched at the edge of my red vinyl chair, and urged me to respond to your second e-mail request for a recommendation, as she dearly hopes to be hired as assistant editor of *Sellebritta Online*.

I demurred. Pressed, I reminded Ms. Tappani that, a year ago, I gave her a well-deserved F in my Intermediate Fiction class. She chuckled and put a manicured little paw on my forearm, as if the two of us were sharing a wonderful joke. "Don't worry about that," she assured me. "I just need a letter."

So be it. Why did I give Ms. Tappani an F? For plagiarizing an entire short story, namely Irwin Shaw's widely anthologized "The Girls in Their Summer Dresses." It always startles me anew—though I have nabbed dozens of plagiarists—to realize that the student cheater is amazed at my powers of discernment, my uncanny ability to detect a difference in quality between his or her own work and, for example, Proust's. I have caught students who faithfully reproduced (or cut and pasted, sometimes forgetting to remove the author's name) the work of Hemingway, Cather, O'Connor (both Frank and Flannery), and Virginia Woolf. The Woolf copyist, wide-eyed with distress and admiration, told me she didn't think I would catch her because Woolf, a European writer no longer among us, was "so obscure."

Back to Ms. Tappani. There is a particular art to accusing a plagiarist, which necessitates first and foremost that I prop my office door open and keep a full box of tissues at hand. But in Ms. Tappani's case the tissues weren't needed. Having confronted her with the Irwin Shaw story prominently featured in several bound volumes on the flat of my desk, I sat back and waited. Visibly unperturbed, she sipped at the froth of a cappuccino. It seemed there was a reasonable explanation. She must have read Shaw's story a few years before. Yes, that must have been it. She had read the story and clearly enjoyed it, to the extent that she had copied it, verbatim, into a notebook reserved for that purpose. Then, finding an assignment due for my class, she had paged through said notebook, stumbled across Shaw's narrative, and forgotten that Shaw, rather than Tara Tappani, was its rightful author. A simple mix-up. She smiled.

I asked if she might show me the notebook into which she copied by hand the works of the masters. Ms. Tappani sighed. She wished that were possible, but only a week earlier she had lost an entire satchel full of journals—including the notebook of literary classics rendered in her own curlicued style—on a city bus. I told her I admired her bravado and gave her the F.

If *Sellebritta Online* is in need of an editor/copywriter who refuses to allow the demands of honesty or originality to delay her output, it will have found one in the unflappable Ms. Tara Tappani.

Guilelessly yours,
Jay Fitger
Professor-at-Law
Creative Writing/English, Payne University

January 14, 2010
Associate Vice Provost Samuel Millhouse
Office of the Vice Provost for Academic Affairs
Lefferts Hall

Dear Associate VP Millhouse,

I write this letter in support of my colleague Karolyi Pazmentalyi in the Department of Slavic Languages, which your office has seen fit to eliminate in its most recent purge. (I am not the only member of the faculty to note that several equally obscure departments, perhaps relieved to have been spared the knife for now, have been gathered together in small ethnic clumps, presumably in preparation for future pogroms.)

Pazmentalyi unfortunately chose this difficult moment in the life of the university to publish the brilliant monograph on which he has been laboring, alone, for the better part of a decade, holed up in a corner of the library, his craggy profile visible in the fluorescent glare of the overheads when everyone else was uncorking a beverage at home. At any other time in the university's history this pathbreaking and exhaustive work of scholarship would immediately elevate its author from the doldrums of associate professordom to the rank of full professor. But now that Slavic Languages is to be summarily flushed down the drainpipe of unprofitable programs and departments (what do we in the Midwest care about Russians, Poles, Serbs, Croatians, Bulgarians, and the denizens of other countries we can't find on a globe or pronounce?), Pazmentalyi is suspended in limbo. He can't be promoted within a department that's being cut; therefore (the logic appears to be), why promote him at all? Why feature photos of bearded brontosauri on the university brag sheets when there are younger, more handsome whizbang faculty (perhaps . . . yes! in the Economics Department!) who will attract more financial interest, instead?

Pazmentalyi, it should be noted, has been reluctant to press or appeal his case. He is the sort of old-fashioned, self-effacing scholar accustomed to hours of painstaking archival research—and, lacking a background as a cage fighter, he will probably take your office's rejection seriously and abide by your suggestion that, forgoing a well-deserved promotion and a minuscule raise, he should lumber off to the newly incorporated "Languages Unit" and soak his head.

But there are other faculty here on campus who are not disposed to see notable scholarship ignored; and let it be known that, in the darkened, blood-strewn caverns of our offices, we are hewing our textbooks and keyboards into spears.

To wit: What would you ask of Pazmentalyi? The reason for denial of his promotion was "narrow scope of research/limited field." Good lord: he's a scholar of Slavic languages—fluent in nearly a dozen—do you want him to coach the volleyball team?* Pazmentalyi is not versatile or charming. He doesn't tell jokes during class. And he won't fight your refusal of his promotion because—brace yourself—he isn't suited for any other job, and he knows it. Very few people read his work; fewer comprehend it. Your office's stated desire for greater "scope" and "accessibility" (would you have Stephen Hawking go back to the nine times table?) will end up turning scholars like Pazmentalyi into TV hosts, forced to incorporate online dating options into seminars previously dedicated to European linguistics.

Faculty acknowledge your need to save money: like most universities, Payne is rapidly pricing itself into oblivion, not by giving modest raises to nationally respected scholars, but by starving some departments while building heated yoga studios and indoor climbing walls in others. To afford the amenities inextricably tied to their education, students need wealthy financial backers or a mountain of loans—and so many on- and off-campus jobs they barely have time to go to class.

Writing this letter has thoroughly depressed me, but it hasn't made me less determined to see Pazmentalyi promoted. You want to sweep out his office and deport him to "Literature" or

* Admittedly, an absurd suggestion: I'm certain the volleyball coach earns three times the salary of a literature professor.

"Cultural Studies" or ask the Mortuary Science Department to find a place for him—so be it. But give him the measly sum he deserves and reward him for superbly performing the work he was hired to do.

Irritated and restless, but not as fractious as I can be,
Jay Fitger
Professor/Agitator/Slum Dweller
Willard Hall

Dear Mr. Young,

Ms. Vanessa Cuddigan has asked me to submit a letter of reference to your poorly spelled organization on her behalf. While I have only praise for Ms. Cuddigan, who graduated two years ago with a major in English, I had expected her to ask that I recommend her for graduate school. Instead, having completed a stint with Teach for America, she is now apparently desirous of some sort of data-entry position with your firm—clearly a soul-squelching enterprise. I have asked her to explain herself but she is evasive, leading me to wonder if something unfortunate happened during the past two years to destroy her ambition.

Should you hire Ms. Cuddigan you will find her thoroughly impressive. She is extremely bright, her insights are fresh, and she has a talent for synthesizing heterogeneous ideas into compelling interpretations of the assigned material. Were she applying to graduate school as I have repeatedly urged her to do, I would take the time here to describe her thesis, a sterling examination of the concept of secrecy in the work of two contemporary novelists, Louise Erdrich and Jonathan Safran Foer, but she has made her Faustian bargain and pinned her newly constricted hopes on Kompu-Metricka, so I will limit myself to recommending her on the basis of her brilliant analytical imagination, her invariable originality of approach, her open-mindedness, and her impeccable character.

You or any other employer will be very fortunate to hire a person such as Ms. Cuddigan, who may one day rise to leadership in your organization, at which point I trust it will adopt a more reasonable spelling. In the meantime, I hope you will not consign her to a windowless environment populated entirely by unsocialized clones who long ago abandoned the reading and discussion of literature in favor of creating ever more restrictive and meaningless ways in which humans are intended to make themselves known to one another.

Keeping the torch aloft, I remain
Jay Fitger
Professor of Creative Writing and English
Author (i.e., books)

Janet:

Sending this in haste and perturbation, and hoping this letter finds you cheerfully disposed toward your onetime spouse . . . I have a graduate student, I believe I told you about him—his name is Browles and he needs a job that will cover his spring tuition. I had hoped to tuck him away for a productive month or two at Bentham, but Eleanor slammed the door in his face, then compounded the insult by offering a *six-month* residency to one of his classmates, a tepid memoir writer named Vivian Zelles. (Please tell me you haven't corresponded with Eleanor about this; have you?)

I appeal not to your long-lost affection for me but your sense of fairness: your law school professors are sitting on tuffets of money over there in Pitlinger, what with old attorneys dying and, graveside, signing over their estates to ensure that every lowly assistant professor gets a research account and a stack of gold bars; here in Willard, on the other hand, the penurious and despondent—with Browles as exemplar—are shuffling back and forth on a stage set from the end of the world.

Janet: Did you know that Madelyne TV died? I just had a letter returned to me from her office, stamped DECEASED. I saw her ten or twelve years ago at a conference in Denver and she looked just the same: that crop of wild hair, the fingers happily cluttered with thick silver rings. I remember her twirling those rings around her fingers at the Seminar table while we waited for HRH's pronouncements, our collective anxiety manifesting itself in the revolutions of those silver bands. It's impossible to think of someone as sparkling as Madelyne ailing and dying; at least she made a valuable life outside academia: working with PTSD sufferers must have been a relief, a step in the direction of clearheaded sanity. Poor sweet lovely TV.

Perhaps your ex-wifely radar has discerned my fatigue. Sometimes when the year grinds to its end and the new term begins I feel I'm living the life of a fruit fly—the endless ephemeral cycle, each new semester a "fresh start" that leads to the same moribund conclusions. I suppose MTV's death has hit me hard—and with Troy reappearing (I wish I knew how to help him) and Eleanor wielding the guillotine at Bentham . . . Well, the timing stings.

In regard to funding for Browles—there's more at stake in this case than support for one student. If he can finish this accursed book and sell it, I can use his success to argue for the continuance—or reinstatement—of our graduate program. Unfortunately, Browles doesn't look the part of the poster child: he can be maddeningly inert, and I just found out that, entirely disregarding my advice, he allowed his registration to lapse. Still, should funding arrive in the guise of a law professor requiring a graduate assistant, I'm sure Carole will manage the reregistration. (After a setback involving an artichoke salad, she's agreed to speak to me again on a limited basis—but only at work between the hours of one-thirty and four.) In case you're worried that, as my protégé, Browles might be writing a novel about Payne or about recognizable people on campus— I assure you, he has better material. Find him a job and he'll work his butt off, and I'll maintain a grateful but dignified distance so that no one in Pitlinger will associate your orotund ex-husband with the new RA.

With the usual regrets and reminiscences,
J

P.S.: Our annual lunch on February 3 at Cava, yes? I'm finished with class at 12:30 . . .

January 25, 2010
Gropp's Liquor Lounge and Winemart
"35 Years of High Spirits"
Dan Stimmson, Proprietor
609 Faygre Avenue
Saint Paul, MN 55101

Dear Mr. Stimmson,

This letter recommends to you my student, Steve Geng, who has applied to Gropp's Liquor Lounge and Winemart in the pursuit of a part-time position. Mr. Geng is a senior here at the university, an English/Spanish double major who finagled his way into an independent study (typically I manage to dodge such requests)—namely, the creation of a mini-anthology of short hallucinatory narratives, each of which begins with a young male speaker (coincidentally named Steve Geng) who has ingested a controlled substance. I believe narrative #1 relies on Adderall, *numero dos* on mushrooms, and #3 on gin.

Comely and articulate, Mr. Geng is prone to dreamy non sequiturs that have endeared him to his peers. I predict that young women will flock to your store in the hopes of hearing him decipher the labels on Chilean and Argentinean wine.

Salud!
Jay Fitger, Professor, Payne University

January 29, 2010
Ken Doyle, Hautman and Doyle Literary Agency
141 West 27th Street
New York, NY 10001

Dear Ken,

You must have heard by now the sad news about MTV: a heart attack, instantaneous—she was fifty-six. Janet and I will raise a glass in her memory at our "divorce anniversary" lunch next week; I wish MTV and I had kept more closely in touch.

In other unnerving Seminar alumni news I've heard from Troy: the poor bastard is back in the U.S. after a decade in India and is scouring the private sector for jobs. The letter I got from him was short and cryptic; it made me envision him living in a canvas tent and washing his underwear in a stream. His only address seems to be a P.O. box. I didn't tell him about MTV, being loath to notify a person with Troy's history about anyone's demise . . . Has he written to you? The idea of a writer with Troy's luminous gifts selling widgets—I find it painful. My intuition tells me he wouldn't have reestablished contact unless he was writing. Put that in your agent's pipe and smoke it.

Which reminds me: the purpose of this letter is actually to recommend to you a student, Vivian Zelles, who read something favorable about you in *Publishers Weekly* and, having learned

93

that you and I were Seminar friends, has waged an implacable daily campaign in my office, insisting that I query you about her work. Zelles is a comparative literature student currently finishing a coming-of-age story purportedly narrated by the first genetically engineered human-feline cross (specifically, a human/cheetah). She began the novel as a memoir, writing about growing up in an immigrant family in California. I found the project to be a bit quiet (that is, dull), which may have led to the manuscript's current confabulation—a pseudo auto-biography in which the speaker portrays herself as a fifteen-year-old girl/cheetah amalgam. Ms. Zelles informs me that the human/animal blend mirrors the false distinction between fiction and fact and points to the necessity of the hybrid form. Whatever the hell she wants to call it—a mem-vel, a nov-oir—the new incarnation of the book is effectively startling, especially the scene in which the protagonist devours and then remorsefully regurgitates her little brother. It's possible, I suppose, that an independent publisher (how many are left, still clinging to their ragged life rafts?) might be intrigued by the project. To that end, the indefatigable Ms. Zelles will be sending, under separate cover next week, an excerpt. See what you think.

Meanwhile I gather—twelve weeks on—you're still mulling Browles's sample? Eleanor spurned him at Bentham (twisting the knife in the wound by admitting Ms. Zelles), after which I asked Janet to arrange for some money to be funneled toward

Browles via an RAship at the law school, but to no avail. Ken— take his sample out of the fucking envelope and read it. Browles doesn't need a big advance; he needs an editor with a functional brain and some vision. (And please refrain from selling the book to the narcoleptics who published *Save Me for Later:* Georgianne is barely sentient, and Simon has forgotten, it seems, how to answer his phone.)

And of course, let me know if you have any interest in Vivian Zelles, whose tabby-infused concoction will cross your desk soon.

Eager, as always, to hear from you,
Jay

P.S.: I need to lodge a belated complaint against the poet— Randolph Marlin—whom I invited to campus in December on your say-so; he was even more of an egomaniac than I expected. Where do poets—with their readership in the low double figures—get off exhibiting that kind of flagrant self-regard? He quizzed the undergrads about his work and then faulted their answers. He wanted to know which of his poems they'd committed to memory. Good god: it was all I could do to restrain myself from saying that my own objective was to try to forget his wretched, soporific lines as completely as possible. I tried to get him drunk at the reception so as to humiliate him for the students' benefit (believe me, they would have been grateful), but he poured four or five glasses of expensive scotch (my tab, of course) down his gullet as if emptying wash water into a drain.

Next time you hand-select a member of your menagerie for a campus visit, make sure she or he is housebroken.

February 2, 2010—Groundhog Day
Addistar Network, Inc.
Bridget Maslow, HR
bmaslow@addistar.com

Dear Ms. Maslow:

Though I prefer to send letters of recommendation via the U.S. Postal Service, now considered by many to be as quaint as muttonchop whiskers and the butter churn, I hereby accede to your request for an e-mail evaluation of Quentin Eshe, who has applied for the position of assistant communications coordinator at Addistar.

Mr. Eshe graduated this past December, a double major in English and phys ed. I can't comment on the phys ed portion of his undergraduate career (what do they study over there? dodgeball?) except to note that Mr. Eshe appears to be physically fit and as tightly coiled as a spring.

As for his English studies: Mr. Eshe was my student in the American Literature Survey and in the Junior/Senior Creative Writing Workshop. He received a B– in the former (I believe he had appendicitis that semester) and an A– in the latter. His final project this past fall was a twenty-page autobiographical essay about his father who, one hopes, will not be permitted to read even a paragraph of the completed work. It is painful and problematic to conclude that another human being—a stranger—does not deserve to be forgiven or loved, but that is the conclusion I drew about Mr. Eshe's father. (His mother is deceased.) Such was the acuity and unflinching vividness of the portrait of the senior Mr. Eshe that I believe I could identify his snarling face in a police lineup.

Eshe is not jovial or loquacious and he won't be the first in your office to set a tray of baked goods by the coffee machine. But by his own account he has survived a difficult if not harrowing childhood; and what skill matters more than the ability to prevail in the face of cruelty, adversity, neglect, and ill will? Furthermore, Mr. Eshe possesses powers of description that, in ways he does not yet recognize or understand, will be of great value to him and others throughout his life.

Given time, Eshe will blossom, and you will be very grateful to have hired him. But do not ask about his family—he has moved on.

Speaking the truth despite its drawbacks, I am
Earnestly yours,
Jason Fitger, Professor of Creative Writing and English
Payne University

P.S.: Belatedly it occurs to me that some members of your HR committee, a few skeptical souls, may be clutching a double strand of worry beads and wondering aloud about the practicality or usefulness of a degree in English rather than, let's say, computers. Be reassured: the literature student has learned to inquire, to question, to interpret, to critique, to compare, to research, to argue, to sift, to analyze, to shape, to express. His intellect can be put to broad use. The computer major, by contrast, is a technician—a plumber clutching a single, albeit shining, box of tools.

February 6, 2010
Portia Jameson, Manager
Xanadu Park RV's
Timothy, MN 55359

Dear Ms. Jameson,

It has come to my attention that your RV park is in need of a (temporary) assistant manager, and I am writing to recommend to you a very mature and responsible individual, Darren Browles. Mr. Browles is soon to be widely known as a novelist, as he is currently putting the finishing touches on a book he has been writing for the past five years. I am sure it would reflect well on your RV park to have an employee—temporary or no—of this impressive stature.

Mr. Browles does not currently own an RV so would require housing while in Xanadu's employ. I do not believe he has any pets and, as per your ad, he is a nonsmoker. Having known him relatively well for the past two years, I can attest to his work ethic, his cleanliness, and his honesty.

With best wishes and anticipating a prompt reply, I am
Jason Fitger, Professor of Creative Writing and English
Payne University

P.S.: Others may have pointed this out to you already but there is no need for an apostrophe in the title of your place of business. Apostrophes are not appropriate for simple plurals; they indicate possession (as in "Darren's book") or the omission of a letter (for example, the absent letter *i* in "Darren's the person we want to hire at Xanadu").

Camilla Mayhew
Chair, Department of English
DiCameron College
55 North Plane Street
Siderea, FL 32703

Dear Camilla,

It seems only a few short years ago that you were here in my office (yes, I am still snugly installed in the same bucolic location, next to the restrooms), asking for a letter of recommendation to assist in what you felt was an unlikely bid for graduate school; and now, post-PhD, with two solid books under your belt, you are already chairing a department. I had faith in you then, and I'm gratified to see that I wasn't mistaken.

You have asked for my candid assessment of Tamar Auden, applicant for the position of assistant professor, tenure track, with concentrations in British literature, rhetoric, and creative writing. And, yes, you are correct in assuming that Dr. Auden was, as an undergraduate, my advisee, though she went on to receive an MA in women's history, an MA in rhetoric/comp, and a PhD in English (her thesis focusing on the Lake poets). But she began as a fiction/fantasy writer, and it was in my classroom where she first sketched out what would become the series of young adult fantasy/sci-fi novels (volume one arriving in bookstores a few months ago) involving a fellowship of teenage aliens who infiltrate a Midwestern boarding school and perform social and intellectual experiments on its hapless young pupils. I suspect the series has inspired you to request this letter—presumably to head off querulousness within your department regarding the potential hire of a "popular" writer. In answer to your unasked questions: yes, I have read the first volume; and no, I am not intending to read volumes two, three, or four—but my lack of enthusiasm for extraterrestrial rapscallions is irrelevant to your search.

Here's the pertinent question: Who in god's name, given the ad your department placed, would argue to turn Dr. Auden down? DiCameron is a small college with limited means: you've clearly been charged with hiring a jack-of-all-trades. And Dr. Auden is that mythical creature you seek: fully qualified to teach British and American literature, women's studies, composition, creative writing, intermediate parasailing, advanced sword swallowing, and subcategories and permutations of the above. As for the aliens: picture the 3-D version of Dr. Auden's first installment, *Experiment Nineteen*, at the multiplex. Has anyone outside the state of Florida heard of DiCameron College? They soon will if you hire Dr. Auden. And consider the financial benefits: she won't need to argue for niggling raises every year, because she'll be earning royalties that will put her faculty salary—and yours—to shame.

I don't mean to be overly facetious, and frankly I salute Dr. Auden and anyone else who can procure a publishing contract during the era of My Personal Screen. The market is forbidding: my own new work has been met with a marked lack of interest by my agent—erstwhile colleague and friend—and most of my backlist is now out of print. (I am reduced to hunting for used copies at the local secondhand store, the proprietor, Alvin, taking sadistic pleasure in stashing my books on a grimy shelf behind the desk, bookmarking the title pages to reveal the inscriptions: *To Devon, in friendship. To Kim: hope to see your own book on these shelves soon! To Carole—Yours always, Jay.*)*

You and your colleagues have nothing to fear from Dr. Auden and her otherworldly teens, who will not spell the demise of Wordsworth and Coleridge: they are dead anyway. Moreover, Dr. Auden is exactly the candidate you are seeking to hire. Working eighty hours per week at a minimum, eschewing hobbies and fitness, she will show up in class with a ribbon of toilet paper unfurling higgledy-piggledy from the sole of her shoe.

* I am always taken aback when students confide in me that beneath their desire to write lies a quest for permanence. It's odd but touching, I think, that even during this disposable age, while consigning great mountains of refuse to landfills and to atolls of plastic in the Pacific, these young would-be novelists and poets believe that art is eternal. Au contraire: we are in the business of ephemera, the era of floating islands of trash, and most of the things we feel deeply and inscribe on the page will disappear.

Her school-uniformed aliens will make her a hit with your students, whom she will lure into your department with the promise of sci-fi—signing them up along the way for any of your low-enrollment classes that require a boost.

Good luck to her and to all of us, Camilla—and congratulations on the tenure-track line. We aren't hiring in the liberal arts at Payne, and as a result I fear we are the last remaining members of a dying profession. We who are senior and tenured are seated in the first car of a roller coaster with a broken track, and we're scribbling and grading our way to the death fall at the top. The stately academic career featuring black-robed professors striding confidently across the campus square is already fading; and, though I've often railed against its eccentricities, I want to proclaim here that I believe our mission and our way of life to have been admirable and lovely, steeped with purpose and worth defending. But we are nearly at the tipping point, I suspect, and will soon be a thing of the past.

How I wish you were sitting at the edge of the red vinyl chair in my office again, twisting the hem of your skirt with your fingers (I'm sure you broke yourself of that habit), asking if I would do you the favor of writing a letter.

Feel free to excerpt this missive before sharing it with other members of your department.

Delighted to have had this chance to be in touch once more, I am pleased to call myself

Your former professor and advisor,

Jason Fitger

Professor of Creative Writing and English

Dear Ms. Gross,

I am referring to your office for the second time, and now with greater urgency, one Wyatt Innes, a member of my Junior/Senior Creative Writing Workshop. I taught Innes a year ago in the American Literature Survey, at which point you may remember I alerted you to his penchant for observing pornography on his laptop during class. To the other students' relief, his attendance faltered, and he eventually failed.

Now he is back, twitching and muttering in a windowless corner of my seminar room, a jumble of notebooks clutched to his chest, and if you could see his rigid, tormented expression you would appreciate how annoying I have found your office's unctuous reminders about the importance of sensitivity to Mr. Innes's and other students' "diverse learning needs." My remaining twenty-nine students' needs presumably include not being terrorized by a psychotic maniac, a person who, in fulfillment of a "character sketch" assignment, turned in forty-five pages of rambling and meaningless gore.

As a professor of creative writing I am thoroughly accustomed to students' depictions of haunted mine shafts, exsanguinations in graveyards, self-mutilation via power tool, sex between gargoyle and human, and illness and torment and abuse of both mundane and incongruous kinds. But Mr. Innes's frenetic rancor is of another order.

I do not sound the alarm lightly, Ms. Gross. Please be advised that, for the second time, I am hereby raising the Flag of Warning; should Mr. Innes initiate a rampage, I will point my finger squarely at you.

Yours in the trenches of academe,
Jay Fitger
Crisis Management Team/Creative Writing Program

February 17, 2010
Maladin IT Associates
Sarah Goodlet, Director, HR
2115 Princeton Avenue
Woodbury, MN 55125

Dear Ms. Goodlet,

Mr. Duffy Napp has just transmitted a nine-word e-mail asking that I immediately send a letter of reference to your firm on his behalf; his request has summoned from the basement of my heart a star-spangled constellation of joy, so eager am I to see Mr. Napp well established at Maladin IT.

As for the basis of our acquaintanceship: I am a professor in an English department whose members consult Tech Help—aka Mr. Napp—only in moments of desperation. For example, let us imagine that a computer screen, on the penultimate page of a lengthy document, winks coyly, twice, and before the "save" button can be deployed, adopts a Stygian façade. In such a circumstance one's only recourse—unpalatable though it may be—is to plead for assistance from a yawning adolescent who will roll his eyes at the prospect of one's limited capabilities and helpless despair. I often imagine that in olden days people like myself would crawl to the doorway of Tech Help on our knees, bearing baskets of food, offerings of the harvest, the inner organs of neighbors and friends—all in exchange for a tenuous promise from these careless and inattentive gods that the thoughts we entrusted to our computers will be restored unharmed.

Colleagues have warned me that the departure of Mr. Napp, our only remaining Tech Help employee, will leave us in darkness. I am ready. I have girded my loins and dispatched a secular prayer in the hope that, given the abysmal job market, a former mason or carpenter or salesman—someone over the age of twenty-five—is at this very moment being retrained in the subtle art of the computer and will, upon taking over from Mr. Napp, refrain (at least in the presence of anxious faculty seeking his or her help) from sending text messages or videos of costumed dogs to both colleagues and friends. I can almost imagine it: a person who would speak in full sentences—perhaps a person raised by a Hutterite grandparent on a working farm.

As for Mr. Napp: you are welcome to him.

Your sincere correspondent,
Jay Fitger
Professor of Creative Writing and English

Salutations, Brian!

Having just learned of KBPZ's recent windfall—every campus radio station should have an aging millionaire alum—I am delighted to come to your aid by recommending for one of your soon-to-be-expanded programs a graduate student and future blockbuster novelist, Darren Browles. Browles is not just a cut above the usual palaverers and symposiarchs of the airwaves; he's three cuts above and would be an ideal anchor for enhanced arts and literature coverage (currently scheduled at an hour when no sane or well-adjusted person is awake to hear it), or for film reviews, or editorial work behind the scenes. Browles is exceptional—bright, articulate, and extremely well read. And in case you're concerned that he might resemble his advisor: be assured that he would sooner elicit others' views than spout his own.

If you could hire him by the end of the month, I'd appreciate it. To be honest, Brian—honesty is my new ambition, a belated New Year's resolution—Browles is in a troublesome place. He owes back rent, he's staggering under his student loans like Atlas with his sphere of the heavens, and I need him to finish this blasted book and sell it so I can argue for the continuance of our graduate program. For god's sake, give him a job that will help him keep the wolf from his door. If I had research money (those days are long gone), I'd pay him to do something: to purge my file drawer of incriminating correspondence or starch and iron my cap and gown. I'll send him over to your office in Butler this week. He may look a bit gaunt (these twenty-somethings love to dress as if each day required their presence at an Irish wake), but I assure you he is diligent, quick, modest, clearheaded, and thorough—and he will be grateful for any manner of work. I'll owe you one, Brian.

Planting yet another bright seed in Payne's fertile soil,
Jay

P.S.: I hope the minor dustup you and I experienced last fall during KBPZ's coverage of the arts fair is well behind us. *I* bear no grudges . . .

Thank you for responding to the Pentalion Corporation's request for a reference for *David Cormier*. Pentalion values confidentiality and will not share your answers to it's inquiries with the applicant.

1. In what capacity and how long have you known the applicant?

David Cormier is an English major and my advisee, due to receive his BA degree at the end of the current semester. I have known him for approximately two years.

2. Describe the applicant's skills and preparedness for a career with Pentalion.

Mr. Cormier, a survivor of my expository writing class, will assuredly not—as the Pentalion Corporation has done above—confuse "its" with "it's," the latter to be used only as a contraction for the two words "it is." Nor will he ever again confuse "lie" and "lay": these are two distinct verbs.

3. Can you think of any reasons why the Pentalion Corporation should not hire the applicant?

Yes. Pentalion is a subsidiary of Koron Chemical, a government contractor known to be a major producer of weaponry used overseas. I would not wish any current or former student to be employed by Pentalion; once *its* leadership masters the basics of punctuation, it should be closed down.

Thank you.

March 1, 2010
Eleanor Acton, *Frau Direktor*
Bentham Literary Residency Program
P.O. Box 1572
Bentham, ME 04976

Dear Eleanor,

Before you consign this letter to the shredder that surely waits, voraciously humming, at the edge of your desk for any sign of correspondence from me, let me assure you that I write today not on my own behalf or that of my "protégé" (your word), but to ask you to create a spot at Bentham for Troy. You saw the William Gass essay in the latest *New York Review of Books*? Gass called Troy's *Second Mind* a "work of acute intelligence, beautifully formed and undeservedly neglected." *WILLIAM. GASS.* I made three copies of the essay and sent them to Troy. I've asked for his street address but he still admits only to the P.O.

Here's my question for you, as director of Bentham: Do you intend to invite Troy for a residency before the literazzi find out how to reach him? Or are you planning to wait until after he's (re)discovered and his dance card is filled? Yes, I know that Bentham residents are admitted or invited based on a written proposal; but Troy is constitutionally incapable of promoting his work, and if you ask him to submit a sample he'll claim he's given up writing, which is completely untrue. Do you remember how self-effacing he was in the Seminar, even with HRH busting his chops—*Mr. Larpenteur, do you have work for us or don't you?* And Troy absently finger tracing a burl in the wooden table, his Tennessee voice soft like thick syrup, *I don't believe I have much to show for myself this week, Reg, I'm not certain yet whether I . . .* until someone threatened to ransack the canvas bag that always slumped like a dog at his feet, at which point Troy would finally distribute a handful of pages. And whatever he had written was un-fucking-believable, we'd reread it later with our mouths half open because he was so brilliant, his work so staggering, he made you want to run your fingers through a table saw and never pick up a pencil again.

In any case, I can assure you he's writing. About a month ago he called me near midnight, and after we went through our usual ritual—I offered to loan him money and he refused—he segued from desultory conversation into a monologue; it took me a moment, but hearing the crinkle of a page I finally understood that he was reading. I listened for forty or forty-five minutes, without comment, and roughly once a week since then we've engaged in similar telephonic performances about which, not being the idiot you believe me to be, I have said nothing: if I spoke, he'd clam up. But I tell you, Eleanor, he is even better than he was before Navia died; he has inscribed his suffering into this work. The piece he read to me a few nights ago was astonishing, crystalline, elliptically structured, an ouroboros devouring its own exquisite tail. The point is: Troy Larpenteur is alive and writing, and with the blessing of William Gass you and Bentham can save him from the anonymous tin enclosure of his P.O. box and be the conduit to his second career. Don't ask him to teach (I doubt he's ready for that); just put him in one of the isolated cabins—the ones near the lake—and let him get his work done.

If you're worried (reasonably so; Troy has always been a perfectionist) that he'll move too slowly and sit on the second book forever, well: you're friendly with his editor—Andrews—at Folkstone, aren't you? He's not speaking to me, for various reasons, but if you were to wave the Gass essay under his nose and tell him that Folkstone needs to reissue *Second Mind* . . . It's much better than the waterlogged tripe they've been publishing lately, and the reissue will stir up interest and give Troy the kick in the pants he'll need to complete the next book. A simple phone call to Andrews, to let him know that Troy is at Bentham and writing again, may be enough.

Should you already be scanning the Bentham date book, about to inform me that every whitewashed cabin is reserved through the millennium, here's news: Vivian Zelles, to whom you offered a six-month stay beginning in July, will be turning you down. She's been admitted to medical school, and she just earned several years' worth of tuition by selling her quasi-memoir, a book in which she narrates her own childhood from the point of view of a sibling-regurgitating feline. She came vibrating into my office yesterday to give me the news. Our old pal Ken sold it for her: six figures.

Do what you can for Troy, will you?

Your problematic onetime colleague,
Jay

P.S.: I sent a note of condolence to MTV's husband, care of Caxton, but the letter came back. Predictable irony: I hadn't spoken to Madelyne for years, but now that she's dead I find there are so many things I'd like to tell her. She and I had an argument once about speculative fiction, and TV claimed that the future didn't interest her, because the proper concern of the writer was always the past. I hope she lived a full life. I wish I had kept in better touch with her and seen it unfold.

March 4, 2010
Galloway Foundation
Research/Travel Awards
27 West 59th Street
New York, New York 10019

Gentle Readers and Committee Members,

My colleague Franklin Kentrell has asked me to recommend him for a Galloway Foundation Research and Travel Award. I would have quickly refused with a clear conscience except that Kentrell penned a Galloway recommendation for me a dozen years ago (I did not receive the award), and in his oily, sidewinding way, he trapped me in the corridor this morning, clutched the lapel of my jacket with his untrimmed nails, and suggested that "tit for tat was only fair."

Kentrell will never survive round #1 of your deliberations; therefore, secure in the knowledge that this letter will soon join thousands of its brethren in a rolling bin destined for recycling—presumably before it is read—I am comfortable endorsing his application.

Wishing you the best of luck with your process,
Jay Fitger
Payne University

March 11, 2010
Ken Doyle
Hautman and Doyle Literary
and Colonic Cleansing Agency
141 West 27th Street
New York, NY 10001

Ken:

I didn't notice your ad for a summer intern (you might have sent it to me), but I have an undergraduate who did: Ms. Daniella Macias is ambitious, intellectually aggressive, yadda yadda yadda, and in light of the mutual reverence with which (I assured her) you and I regard each other, she has already lined up a summer sublet in Brooklyn for herself and an elderly diabetic cat. Given the pay scale (you're not paying *anything*?), I assume you'll be glad to have her around. She won't expect you to hand over your winningest clients; she just wants to soak up some atmosphere and dip her beggar's tin cup into your font of wisdom.

On another topic: congratulations on the Big Sale. Six figures! Apparently I need to reinvent myself as a debut novelist, preferably young, beautiful (has Vivian sent you her photo?), and en route to med school. I confess I hadn't expected it (perhaps I should have, given public enthusiasm for the teratological and the macabre)—but, kudos! Once you've finished with the champagne toasts I hope you'll remember on whose say-so Vivian sent you her work; you might even decide to take your seven-hundred-dollar shoes off the desk and reconsider your opinion of Browles—which was crude and slapdash, Ken; the book is not a "turgid, pedestrian belaboring of a minor classic." The first hundred pages may drag a bit: I'll tell Browles to streamline and send them back to you as soon as he's done.

Finally, I'm sure you're plugged into the hype about Troy: *The New York Review of Books*'s ecstasies, a forthcoming residency at Bentham (or so I've heard—but don't quote me as your source), and the long-awaited second book under way . . . Is he going to lone-wolf it again, or have you persuaded him to take you on this time as his agent? I suppose if you brokered a repub at Folkstone he might view you favorably, and more fully understand your agently charms . . .

Daniella Macias's earnest little résumé will probably be on your desk by the time you read this—give her a chance, will you?

Speculatively,
Jay

P.S.: Janet sent me the note you wrote to the alumni website about MTV. You're right: she was a candle.

P.P.S.: Where does the time go?

The Ides of March
Office of the Provost/Attention: Dean Rensselear
Shepardville College
88 Cordry Hall
Tumbling Springs, GA 30350

Dear Dean Rensselear:

Carole Samarkind has asked that I submit this letter of recommendation on her behalf, as she is applying for your associate dean of student affairs position; with great regret I comply. The prompt in your online form (which I am ignoring in favor of this more accurate anachronism of a letter) asks that in addition to addressing Ms. Samarkind's qualifications, I evaluate her past and current performance, disclose the context in which I know her, and discuss her liabilities (if any) and her future promise.

I. Past and Current Performance
Ms. Samarkind has served steadily, diplomatically, magnificently in the Student Services/Fellowship Office here at Payne University for eleven years. She is an enviable constant in the chaotic and demanding environment in which she tactfully holds sway, managing to advocate for student welfare, calm the neuroses of the faculty, and assuage the bilious and unpredictable tempers of the myriad deans (I have often pictured her

stage-managing a fashion show of monsters) with whom she has, for over a decade, worked.

II. Context of My Acquaintanceship with Ms. Samarkind

Carole and I slept together—without cohabiting or making promises we would be unable to honor—for almost three years. Though we met via the many letters of recommendation I sent to her on behalf of my students (an odd sort of wooing, consisting as it had to of my praise for others), we came face-to-face, I believe, for the first time when I stormed into her office to protest the dissolution of an undergraduate award, which had been advertised, applied for, and then withdrawn. I had expected Ms. Samarkind to be an officious group-thinking gorgon who would proffer a bushel of vapid excuses by way of toeing the university's line; instead, she listened, then agreed that the discontinuance of the award was unfair and quickly saw to its restitution.

Our years of tumbling in the hay began, if memory serves, soon after that. Apologies for the candor—which, as dean of what was recently known as a Bible college, you may experience as a bit of a shock—but I assure you these personal comments are entirely relevant. Why is Ms. Samarkind applying to Shepardville College? At the risk of revealing myself to be an egotist, I submit that I figure prominently into her decision. Let's consider the facts: Carole is comfortably installed at a research university—dysfunctional, yes; second tier, without question—

but we do have a modest reputation here at Payne. Shepard-ville, on the other hand, is a third-tier private college teetering at the edge of a potato field and is still lightly infused with the tropical flavor of offbeat fundamentalism propagated by its millionaire founder, a white-collar criminal who is currently—correct me if I'm wrong—atoning for multiple financial missteps in the Big House in Texas. You've reinvented yourselves and gone secular, but clearly, in various pockets and odd recesses of the campus, glassy-eyed recidivists and fanatics are still scream-ing hosannas, denying the basic tenets of science, and using a whetstone to sharpen their teeth.

III. Liabilities

I would argue that Carole's are limited to her three-year blind spot with me. Obviously I failed her rather than vice versa; I was ruminative, churlish, and illiberal regarding endearments and other attentions. Just past the two-and-a-half-year mark, she accused me of being in love with my despotic ex-wife—one does not, after all, twist affection closed like a spigot—and though I denied it, Carole had discovered in me, or more accu-rately in my writing (I should not have inscribed and allowed her to read *Transfer of Affection*), a love of conflict, a fondness for rivalry both sexual and literary that pointed toward a ves-tigial tenderness and susceptibility to my ex-wife's adamantine charms. In short, I was disloyal and selfish. And it is my con-tinuing selfishness—my desire to maintain for my own and the university's benefit an exceptional human being and employee like Carole—that allows me to include in this letter all the things it contains.

IV. Future Promise

Ms. Samarkind's stellar administrative skills, as detailed on her résumé, are enhanced by intelligence, tact, steadfastness, optimism, kindness, perseverance, and unwavering good sense. Your institution may gain her—depending on how fervently she hopes to insert some miles between us—but there is nothing Shepardville can possibly do to deserve her.

With candor, regret, and a whiff of vengeance, I am
Jay Fitger, Professor of Creative Writing and English
Payne University
Author, *Stain; Alphabetical Stars; Save Me for Later;* and *Transfer of Affection*

cc: Carole Samarkind. (Carole: I didn't think it was fair to send this without cc'ing you. Hate me if you like—you're too good for Shepardville and both you and they know it.)

Dear Ted,

Obediently complying with your latest summons for superfluous information, I am, yes, thoroughly willing to recommend Arabella McCoy for the position of teaching assistant mentor, her duties to begin midsummer, a period of time during which, one can only hope, the poisonous vapors seeping through the vents in Willard Hall will have dispersed, and the economists, scepters agleam, will be reinstalled in their throne rooms over our heads, emerald chalices raised in a grand *huzzah!* for the coronation. You understand of course that Ms. McCoy is a stranger to me: I may have glimpsed her in the hall, poor burdened wight, as she trudged from one lecture to another in her yard-sale clothes, thick piles of yet-to-be-graded undergraduate essays under a rawboned arm; but mainly, as required, I have skimmed her CV and her letter of interest, both of which express the requisite theater-of-the-absurd language about pedagogy and the euphoria of learning. Suffering creature! By all means, yes, yes! I endorse her bid for the mentorship: may the bump in salary allow her to avoid scurvy by adding fruit to her diet once a week.

While we're on the important topic of health: there must be something you can do, Ted, about the thick coils of tubing that, as of yesterday, emerged from a sizeable hole in the wall outside my office. Resembling the heads of a modern-day Hydra, these tubes periodically cough up flocculent curds of unidentifiable gray material, as if issuing a warning to those who remain in Willard Hall.

Sometimes in my daydreams, Ted, I envision our building in a cutaway view as if it were a painting by Hieronymus Bosch: the economists placidly robed in the uppermost quadrant, nearest to God, and beneath them, on the lower floors, close to the churning wrath of the boiler, the condemned in a bloodstained, pulsing version of Hell.

I'm sure Ms. McCoy will be an apt and responsible mentor.

Extracting pleasure from the task as always,
Jay

March 19, 2010
Reverend W. T. Dap, Admissions
Emanuel Lutheran Seminary
Corcoran, SD 57106

Dear Reverend Dap,

Dennis White has asked me to write a letter recommending him to the Emanuel Lutheran Seminary (Master of Divinity Program), and I am happy to grant his modest request. Four years ago Mr. White enrolled as a dewy-eyed freshman in one of my introductory literature courses (Cross-cultural Readings in English, or some such dumping ground of a title); he returned several years later for another dose of instruction, this time in the Junior/Senior Creative Writing Workshop—a particularly memorable collection of students given their shared enthusiasm for all things monstrous and demonic, nearly every story turned in for discussion involving vampires, werewolves, victims tumbling into sepulchres, and other excuses for bloodletting. I leave it to professionals in your line of work to pass judgment on this maudlin reveling in violence. A cry for help of some sort? A lack of faith—given the daily onslaught of news about melting ice caps, hunger, joblessness, war—in the validity or existence of a future? Now in my middle fifties, an irrelevant codger, I find it discomfiting to see this generation dancing to the music of apocalypse and carrying their psychic burdens in front of them like infants in arms.

Mr. White concentrated in his fiction not on poltergeists and phantoms but on the potential for evil within. In his final story, the intriguingly yclept main character, Davin Dark, falls into a trance during which he kills his younger brother, then wakes to the horrid evidence of what he has done. Despite a problem with modifiers, the story was genuinely disturbing, and I found myself recalling its eerie details whenever Mr. White—a handsome, smooth-browed young man—raised his hand in class. And now you ask whether Mr. White is a compelling candidate for the seminary; whether a person whose literary subconscious is an autoclave aboil with fratricide and vice is fit to serve as the moral shepherd of anyone's flock.

In weighing in on this question I have to confess to my own status as a nonbeliever. Episcopalian* as a child, I wandered listlessly away from the fold in college. Years later, my wife (we are now divorced; I cheated on her, but that's a story for another time) entertained cozy connubial visions of the two of us joining a congregation of Unitarians. Unfortunately, to my spiritually untutored mind, the contemplation of the infinite and the cultivation of virtue required the dignity of flowing robes and incense—whereas the Universalists eschewed pageantry and tradition so completely they might

* Mainly because my mother believed that Episcopalian women dressed better than Catholics, and I suspect she was right.

as well have met for worship at a rodeo. As for me, the closest I have come to exaltation has been here at the university, with a book in my hand. Literature has served me faithfully (no pun intended) as an ersatz religion, and I would wager that the pursuit of the ineffable via aesthetics in various forms has saved as many foundering souls as a belief in god.

Forgive the tirade. My point: you are searching for an intellectually and morally fit young person, presumably one with leadership ability, empathy, integrity, an inquiring nature, and rhetorical skills. To the best of my knowledge, all of the above reside in Mr. White, in whom you will also find a restless attraction to the inexplicable, to loss and sadness and cruelty, to fear. I am willing to go out on a proverbial limb here for Mr. White—I can feel myself beginning to advocate for him more strongly as I type these words—and predict that his penchant for dybbuks and nightmares might one day assume the shape of a search for grace.

Mr. White is not yet a candle ready to illuminate anyone else's darkness, but he understands that the darkness exists, and he does not turn away.

I beg your indulgence for this overlong letter, which clearly betrays its author's own internal struggles (especially piquant at this time of year, with its leaden sky and its slag heaps of snow) and concludes by highly recommending Mr. White to you, your colleagues, and your institution.

In ambiguity and continuing the search,
J. T. Fitger, Professor of English and Creative Writing
Payne University

March 22, 2010
Rene DeClerc, Chair
Department of Politics and Government
11 Tenafield Hall West

Dear Rene—

Louise Frame is applying for the position of associate administrator in your department; happily, I am able to recommend her to you without reservation and with a clear conscience. Ms. Frame has served as associate administrator in the Department of English for nineteen years (I remember when she arrived, fresh faced and vibrant, having no idea of the devastating environment into which she had come); she is fully adept at accounts and billing; she is responsible and highly professional (the young man who will undoubtedly rise through the ranks to replace her in our unit dresses like a sanitation worker); and she has taken only three sick days (three!) in the past eight years.

Typically in a letter such as this one, it behooves the writer to address the applicant's motive or incentive to seek a new job. We both know that shouldn't be necessary in this case: one can only interpret a desire to exit the Department of English as a mark of sound judgment. It is an indication of Ms. Frame's loyalty to Sarah Lempert (now retired—she chaired for eight of Louise's nineteen years) that it took her so long to decide to go.

Poor Ms. Frame is too discreet an employee to reveal the particular absurdity or humiliation that tipped the scales and persuaded her to seek reassignment: it might have been the fisticuffs in the lounge over the issue of undergraduate curriculum, or the faculty meeting (Ms. Frame faithfully taking minutes) during which a senior colleague, out of his mind over the issue of punctuation in the department's mission statement, threatened to "take a dump" (there was a pun on the word "colon" which I won't belabor here) at a junior faculty member's door.

We have long vied for recognition as the most dysfunctional of departments (Psychology, of course, with "Madman" Tollson at the helm has generally been first); now, with a paper-pushing outsider (Ted B.) as chair, we are living in a Brave New Department, in a building half of which has been cordoned off with tape as a hazardous zone. Those of us who remain in Willard Hall abandon the relative safety of our offices only to tiptoe into the hallway to use the restroom. (In fact, one member of the department has created his own intra-office relief station— but I will spare you those details or offer them up at a more opportune time.)

In sum, Louise Frame is an exemplary employee. Take pity on her, throw her a lifeline, and allow her to dry herself off among friends.

From the prow of the *Titanic,*
JTF

Dear Reg,

After some effort, I believe I have tracked you down at the above address. I hope you're well. I was sorry to hear about the stroke (news of your retirement traveled in seismic shivers through the daily papers), and I can appreciate your desire for privacy as well as rest. I wouldn't bother you on my own behalf: I'm writing for the benefit of and unbeknownst to my advisee, Darren Browles, truly a diamond in the rough and one of the most original student writers I have encountered in the twenty-two years since I graduated, grateful for everything you did for me, from the Seminar.

Briefly: Browles's funding at Payne has been cut by the technocrats who have lately seized power over this institution, and he can't afford to finish his degree or—more crucially—his novel, currently titled *For the Sake of a Scrivener.* Remembering how crucial your support of *Stain* was for me, I'm taking the liberty of enclosing several of Browles's chapters: I'm hoping you can peruse them, see the raw potential, and use your influence—either to connect Browles with an agent (Ken Doyle is not the right fit for this project) or to recommend that he be admitted, belatedly and with funding (and I know it's not the same now, without you), to the Seminar.

You might logically suggest that the easier route would be to send Browles to Bentham. I've already tried: I wrote him an over-the-top letter, but Eleanor has rejected him repeatedly, despite or because of my panegyrics. Her rancor is personal and dates back to *Stain:* she claimed that my object in writing the novel was humiliation—specifically, that I made her the unwilling model for my character, Esther, and that the sex scenes in the book (though I did eliminate one of the most lurid) too nearly depicted the stormy liaison in which we briefly engaged. She said your enthusiasm for *Stain* was misogynistic—and that it was vanity and a "puppeteer's obsession with control" that led you to help me win that first publication. My ex-wife, Janet (I'm sure you remember her: you described her work as "unrealized" and "sterile"), origi-nally dismissed Eleanor's complaints as overreaction. She pointed out that the book wouldn't have gone into paperback and a third printing if its only attribute was the embarrassment of a former flame. Now that we are divorced, Janet sympathizes with Eleanor; they correspond. As for *Stain:* how excruciating two decades later, those blowsy fanfaronades of the prose; and who is that beady-eyed intense young author with the full head of hair?

I'm not asking for eleventh-hour honesty here: you were a terrific advisor, whether you believed in what I was writing or whether—amused by *Stain*'s teasing references to the intimate lives of those who gathered around you at the Seminar table—you viewed my work as an experiment, a test of your influence, both on me and the market. The outcome for me, no matter your motive, was the same, and in either case, I am grateful. Though most of my work is out of print (perhaps deservedly so, in regard to *Save Me for Later* and *Alphabetical Stars*), *Stain* secured me a job, a tenured position that many would envy. (My pre-Seminar career involved the sale of cleaning products from the back of a Chevy Chevette.) Still, I feel a moment of reckoning approaching. My own writing interests me less than it used to; and while I know that to teach and to mentor is truly a calling, on a day-to-day basis I often find myself over-whelmed by the needs of my students—who seem to trust in an influence I no longer have, and in a knowledge of which, increasingly, I am uncertain—and by the university's mindless adherence to bureaucratic demands.

I'm sure you have your own frustrations, but if there's anything you can do for Browles, any assistance similar to that which, twenty-two years ago, you extended to me, I would so appreci-ate the favor. Please note that I'm enclosing these pages from his proposal and his opening chapters without his knowledge; unlike his advisor, Browles does not advocate for himself and is an unassuming man.

Thank you, Reg. Still gazing up at you on that pedestal, fondly, Jay

March 29, 2010
Amis and Portman Associates
165 South First Avenue
Baxton, MI 48103
Attention: Mary T. Radziwill

Dear Ms. Radziwill:

Abhinav Mehta has requested that I send a letter of recommendation to your firm on his behalf and, though I am supposed to
be enjoying the one-week hiatus known and dreaded in vacation spots across the globe as "spring break," I am happy to do
so; but I have encountered several obstacles. The first is that Mr.
Mehta, despite the desperate language in which he couched
his desire for me to attend to this letter with the utmost speed,
no longer responds to his university e-mail or phone, and did
not deign to inform me of the position for which he is applying. Such are the communication skills of the up-and-coming
generation: they post drunken photos of themselves at parties,
they share statuses, they emit tweets and send all sorts of intimate pronouncements into the void—but they are incapable of
returning a simple phone call. Second, my inquiry to your firm,
Amis and Portman, fails to shed any light on the subject of a
possible hire. Your website requests that I load particular soft-
ware into my own irregularly functioning computer (no, I will
not), and your answering service functions as an impenetrable
barrier, insisting that I press, in numeric form, the first three let-

ters of the last name of the individual to whom I wish to speak. I tried entering a few letters at random, but to no avail.

I can offer you some informative tidbits should Mr. Mehta resurface for the (unspecified) job with your mysterious firm:

1. Mr. Mehta received a final grade—in my Junior/Senior Creative Writing Workshop—of B+, having completed a short story about a cannibal couple, husband and wife, who find themselves stranded and hungry by a fire pit after a cave-in. Intended to be philosophical rather than humorous, the story nevertheless succeeded in great comic effect.

2. Mr. Mehta's transcript may give the erroneous impression of indolence, given that he stitched his education together like a crazy quilt over a period of six years. In Mr. Mehta's defense, I know that he worked almost full-time and had multiple problems with his student loans—byzantine snafus that prevented him from registering on time for required classes. Suffice it to say that I could run the Office of Financial Aid at this institution more efficiently on the back of a dirty envelope than the current dean, with his cabal of neurotic misfits, has managed to do.

Should your firm and Mr. Mehta abandon your respective cloaks of anonymity and locate each other, I believe you will be reasonably satisfied with his organizational and writing skills.

In camera obscura,
J. Fitger, Professor, Creative Writing and English

Dear Janet,

I know you aren't on the search committee for the adminis-trative assistant position, but to hell with protocol: you're the only person I know or trust in the law school, everyone under-stands that you're pulling the strings over there (your decision to divorce me having increased the esteem in which most staff and faculty hold you), and I'm counting on your willingness to respond to this LOR, because the situation is dire.

Who am I recommending? Louise Frame. You remember Lou-ise from my earlier years in Willard Hall; I believe you once described her as an island of hospitality in the heart of darkness of the department. You may have heard that she accepted the administrative job in Political Science: true, she did, and she hap-pily said yes to their larger salary—but three or four days ago her meth-addict daughter cruised into town just long enough to deposit on Louise's doorstep a two-year-old whose name is X. Not Xerxes or Xavier, but the letter X, a silent, emotion-ally scarred creature summarily abandoned in Louise's kitchen without a suitcase or a toy or clothes. An act of hideous neglect, yes; but according to Louise, given the shape her daughter was in, it was also, possibly, an attempt at redemption and an act of kindness—a second chance for her son.

So. The Poli-Sci job is full-time, and you know those spreadsheet-loving barbarians will work her to death; and because of X having parachuted into her life (he doesn't yet speak, or she hasn't heard him do so), Louise needs two months off, minimum, after which you know she'd be the ideal associate administrator you're looking for, efficient and smart and organized—but you must give her benefits with a 75-percent-time position and match her Poli-Sci salary (the law school can easily afford it) because of the child. I suggested that she make an appointment to see you and she completely broke down. And don't tell me she should come back to English: the latch on that door has clicked shut behind her; we've already hired a semicompetent aphasic at less than half of Louise's pay.

Perhaps it's a godsend you and I never had a child.

Did I tell you I wrote to HRH? You may find that a ludicrous gesture, but it occurred to me that he might use his (waning) influence to benefit Browles.* And, by the by, where does Eleanor get off, telling you that Browles's *Bartleby* excerpt was "an

---

* As for your suggestion that Browles appeal for emergency funding to the grad student council: that body is commandeered, as per usual, by a group of unshaven Stalinists—still, I passed the idea along.

unholy mess"? He hasn't had adequate time to revise, and he feels like an orphan now that the safety net of the graduate program's benefits is being sliced out from under his feet. Say what you like about the Seminar: we were all funded back then, and we may not have lived high on the hog, but neither were we plunged into financial crisis. I tell you, Janet, I am becoming soft and sentimental; I spend more and more time thinking back to the group of us hungering around HRH and the Seminar table: our yearning kept us alive and enriched us. And now that our bowls have been filled and we've been sent off with our dollops of gruel—what enriches us now?

I so enjoyed our lunch back in February. It was good to hear that you're writing again. I have a vision of myself from the early days of our marriage, hunched like a bullfrog at the paint-splattered table overlooking the Welligers' garage, concocting a supposed work of genius and barely mumbling an acknowledgment when you knocked at the door to tell me you were going to accept the job at the law school. You'd sealed your manuscript into a series of manila envelopes and filed them on a shelf in the closet. And there I was, typing like a madman (I used to allow myself a shot of Prairie Vodka after every five pages; I should have smacked my skull with a plank instead), imagining myself a Brilliant Young American Novelist. Ha. Ha. Ha.

Could we schedule an additional lunch this year? Why should we limit ourselves to two?

Louise promised me she would contact you ASAP. Prepare yourself: She used to be stoic and unruffleable, but given the arrival of X (I've urged her to file for a birth certificate and lengthen his name), she has become a weeper. Keep an eye on the trembling lower lip.

Forever your ex-spouse,
Jay

P.S.: How did you end up with a copy of the LOR I wrote for Carole, to Shepardville? I agree it was somewhat draconian—and I've tried to apologize to Carole, but she won't answer my e-mails and no longer allows me into her office. Realistically, though: Was I supposed to stand by, twiddling my thumbs, while on my account she threw her career down the toilet? If my LOR outraged you so much, I suppose you could write her a letter yourself. But would Carole interpret that gesture as solidarity? Or as your own (subconscious) desire to see her leave town?

Peter B. Andrews, Executive Editor
Folkstone Publishing
26 Ulysses Avenue, Suite B
Chicago, IL 60618

Dear Peter Andrews,

In response to your e-mail query received this morning, I'm delighted to endorse Ken Doyle's recommendation that Folkstone reissue Troy Larpenteur's exquisite debut, *Second Mind*. *Second Mind* was an underappreciated landmark when Folkstone took a chance and premiered it almost seventeen years ago; now, of course, it's a cult classic, copies of which are jealously traded and difficult to find. I thoroughly agree with Ken's suggestion regarding the William Gass remarks—they should be prominently displayed on the front cover—and the reuse of H. Reginald Hanf's original blurb on the back. You might also solicit a paragraph of praise from Eleanor Acton, who has, as you probably know, offered Troy a coveted teaching-free residency at Bentham. And finally, yes, I can vouch for academic interest in the book, which will be assigned here at Payne and at other universities in both creative writing and contemporary literature classes.

Folkstone's timing on this reissue is truly fortuitous: Troy's long-awaited and groundbreaking second volume (sworn to secrecy about its content, I've read only a few remarkable excerpts) will more than live up to and increase the buzz surrounding his first.

Please keep me apprised as to the (re)publication schedule, as I generally complete larger orders of required books for classroom use three months ahead, and let me know if there is anything I can do to help promote the work of this very talented man.

With genuine as well as vicarious pleasure,
J. Fitger, Professor of Creative Writing and English
Payne University
Author, *Stain; Alphabetical Stars; Save Me for Later;* and *Transfer of Affection*

Dear Ms. Gross,

Having disposed of the budding psychopath, Mr. Wyatt Innes, I am sending to your office with this letter in hand a human bath of tears named Ida Lin-Smith, who tells me she called your office for an appointment and was turned away. I did not inquire as to her malady, but a simple glance in her direction suffices to inform me that she requires attention. Please offer her something more lasting and substantial than guided breathing or twenty minutes with a golden retriever.

I sometimes wonder, Ms. Gross, about the source of such widespread unhappiness. I imagine a manufactory of anxiety and sorrow belching out clouds of discontent on the north side of campus. (Some miseries, of course, are self-inflicted. You are probably aware of my e-mail fiasco at the end of last summer, my "reply to all" message disclosing to every member of the faculty, staff, and administration my desire to rekindle a relationship with my ex-wife, Janet Matthias—a blunder that inspired the good Carole Samarkind to sever forever our romantic ties. I am increasingly prone to mistakes of this sort, ·

perhaps because of the ticker tape of LORs that travels ceaselessly through my pen. *Please admit this woman into your program. Please give this unsocialized person some funding. Please offer this mediocre student a chance to improve his condition. Pleasepleasepleaseplease.*)

Never mind, Ms. Gross. I advocate here for the lachrymose Ms. Lin-Smith—still weeping patiently in my office chair—and not for myself. I am fine, I assure you.

Yours in this watery chasm,
Professor Jay Fitger

Theodore Boti, *Kapellmeister* and Chair
Department of English

Dear Ted,

In response to your clarion call for nominations for the four-hundred-dollar summer research fellowship for undergraduate majors (can't we locate some wealthier donors? over in the business school, bronze plaques are crowded with the names of benefactor alums), I hereby forward the application of Gun-nar Lang.

Lang has done a knock-up job in the department this year, mastering the enigmas of copying, stapling, and filing; furthermore, you may recall that he was nearly decapitated back in December by a chunk of plaster that fell from the ceiling onto the fax machine while he was standing beside it—this only twenty-four hours after the engineers chuckled away our anxieties about the crevasse that had opened like a kraken's mouth above the mailroom door.

Lang is proposing next year to produce an exegesis of Tim O'Brien's *In the Lake of the Woods;* if awarded the funds he will presumably put them to use in July and August by availing himself of the foul-smelling vending machine sandwiches in Appleton Library while immersing himself in a study of narrative uncertainty and violence: a summer well spent. Furthermore, Lang is unflappable about the near beheading and has not yet sued us. The four hundred dollars seems a small price to pay for his silence.

I can vouch for Lang's integrity, having seen him deposit fifty cents in the till in exchange for the liquid our department elects to call coffee. (Franklin Kentrell, on the other hand, has been known to regard the coffee till as a personal scholarship fund for his lunch.)

Please bestow the fellowship on Lang.

Signing off with the usual commitment to righteousness and justice,
Jay Fitger, Winner's Circle
American Letter of Recommendation Society

P.S.: I assume it was someone's idea of a joke to insert in the minutes from last week's budget meeting the idea of my serving as associate chair? Given your three-year mandate to "turn English around," I presumed that—if you needed assistance quelling the rabble—you'd search for some hapless junior faculty member who lacked the clout to refuse. As for me, I am probably the least likely associate chair you could find. No one would listen to me; I seldom listen to myself.

April 23, 2010
Leticia Alistair
Flanders Nut House
771 Glass Lake Road
Glass Lake, WI 54153

Dear Ms. Alistair,

This letter recommends to you my student, Oliver Postiglione, who informs me that he has applied for a summer job at Flanders Nut House at the south end of Glass Lake. In a strange coincidence, I spent one summer—during my teenage years, but indelibly impressed upon me—in the timeless village of Glass Lake; and as if I were at this very moment standing on the cracked sidewalk in front of it, I can envision the screen door of the Nut House slapping shut in the breeze and recall the smell of my favorite purchase, the roasted almonds wrapped, still warm and lightly salted, in a paper cone. I hope for the sake of Mr. Postiglione's dignity your establishment no longer requires its most junior employee to dress as a human cashew.

You will want to ascertain that Mr. Postiglione is trustworthy, hardworking, and of pleasant affect: he is all three. A member of my Junior/Senior Creative Writing Workshop, he is currently writing a one-act play about a serial killer/scientist who saves humankind from a world-ending virus by discovering a method of harvesting corpses to create a vaccine. The concept is gruesome and not very original, but Mr. Postiglione's workmanlike approach to the project's completion is to be admired.

I hope the gold lettering continues to grace the façade of the Nut House, its broad front window perfectly reflecting the water's stillness. Though I have not returned to Glass Lake for forty years, one never forgets the places in which one felt pure.

As for Mr. Postiglione: he will learn quickly, whether waiting on customers behind the pristine white tile counter or assisting with packages in back. I recommend him to you warmly and without hesitation, in part because writing letters of reference such as this one allows me to reinhabit, if only fleetingly, the pensive, knock-kneed person I once was and to advocate for that former version of myself as well as for Oliver Postiglione. Please do hire him; I wish him episodes of glorious, sun-washed tedium and a loss of innocence he will contemplate for the rest of his life.

Commemoratively,
Jason T. Fitger
Professor of Creative Writing and English
Payne University

April 29, 2010
Philip Hinckler, Dean
College of Arts and Sciences
1 MacNeil Hall

Dear Dean Hinckler,

Firmly situated between the proverbial rock and its opposing hard place, I am in this letter recommending that your office, in its infinite wisdom, renew and continue the provisional appointment of Theodore Boti, social scientist cum litterateur, as English Department chair. In my wildest nightmares I never imagined that I would make or endorse such a recommendation, akin to Hamlet naming Uncle Claudius counsel (*Hamlet* is a play by a writer named William Shakespeare; I'll send you a copy on some other occasion)—but these are desperate and difficult times.

Mindful of your office's infatuation with all things pithy and straightforward,* I offer below a cogent list of reasons why Boti—duck out of water that he is—should continue as chair.

---

* I recall your witticism at the provost's reception last year: that as much as you detested my LORs, you found them more engaging than any of my novels, which you dismissed as "ponderous."

1. A single year of any administrative responsibility is pointless. Boti hasn't yet reached the first fat dot on the learning curve. As chair, he will most likely fail—after which my colleagues and I will condemn him—but subsequent to a traditional three-year term, our condemnation and Boti's failure will be seen to occur on more solid ground.

2. In the context of the hiring freeze—purportedly imposed on all departments but inflicted mainly on English and the Lilliputian units—and in light of our diminution via recent retirements, we can't afford to sacrifice even one teaching colleague to the funeral pyre of administration. You want undergraduates who can write, think, and read? Stop pretending that writing can be taught across the curriculum by geologists and physicists who wouldn't recognize a dependent clause if it bit them on the ass.

3. Boti's a sociologist. And yes, sociology has gone the way of poli-sci and econ, now firmly in the clutches of rabid number crunchers who have abandoned or forgotten the link between their abstruse theoretical musings and the presence of human beings on the planet's surface; still, Boti was a student once, drawn during some primeval past to the study of human communities and social organizations, and as such he is likely to possess an albeit long-buried interest in the operation of a collective. If nothing else, he may get an academic paper out of the experience (though who'd want to read it?).

4. Boti loves protocol and detail. Your office loves protocol and detail. Nuff said.

5. Finally and perhaps most important: despite himself, Boti lately evinces an incipient understanding of the dilemmas of our woebegone department, and this dawning knowledge may eventually lead him to advocate for its health and well-being. Witness, for example, his mild amazement when informed that English has shrunk in the past eight years by more than 20 percent. See the wrinkle in his snowy brow upon learning that our student fellowships have been slashed, our graduate programs defunded, our classroom sizes increased, our faculty research and travel funds canceled, the student literary journal paid for by donations collected on street corners in aluminum cans, and on and on. You may have intended his installation as outside chair as a punitive wake-up call for our department, but I am not sure the arrangement has resulted as planned.

In an unguarded moment, Boti expressed surprise at what he termed our faculty's "docile disengagement." I informed him that we are like oxen accustomed to the yoke: our hides thick from insult and whippings, we have forgotten how to do anything other than trudge dully along.

Even more: Having spent his tenure-seeking years in the gleaming spaceship of Atwell Hall, Boti—like a wealthy traveler touring the slums—is suitably horrified by the state of our building, with its intermittent water supply, semioperational light fixtures, mephitic odors, and corridors foggy with toxins. Yesterday, on the metal bookshelf in my office, I came across a cluster of insects—a beetle, two moths, a centipede, and several bluebottle flies—writhing together like dirgeful companions in their final death throes, presumably poisoned by vapors from the second floor. But never mind: I am sure our foreshortened life spans will be made worthwhile on the day when the economists, in their jewel-encrusted palanquins, are reinstalled in their palazzo over our heads. (Climbing the stairs and peering into their future home yesterday, I found that the double doors leading to their sanctuary are equipped with locks—presumably to prevent riffraff and English faculty from getting in.)

Enfin: With mixed feelings (but what feelings aren't mixed, when one is a professor of the humanities?), I put my shoulder to the wheel for Boti: give him two more years.

As for the rumor that, Boti unwilling (I assume you are tempting him with previously undiscovered funds), I might be counted among the eligible candidates to serve in his place—I consider it both ludicrous and unsound. Why? Because the upper echelons of the administration justifiably detest me; because my colleagues view me as a cantankerous pariah; and because, given my stance on several university-wide issues, I would consider the position a significant ethical and even spiritual compromise—and I say that as an agnostic. Ergo: Assuming that the rumor isn't a joke expressly devised for my humiliation, you may color me

Flattered but uninterested,
Jay

Dear Ted,

You have asked me—for the third time this year—to submit a letter of recommendation for Franklin Kentrell, applicant/supplicant for the Citrella Service Award.

You requested that I leave out "all extraneous information," limiting myself to statements associated with my endorsement of Kentrell's (self-)nomination.

. . .

Thank you for this opportunity to express so thoroughly my feelings on this crucial subject.

Elliptically,
Jay

P.S.: I assume you're demurring on the reappointment for chair in order to bargain for something. Might the Overlords be persuaded to fork over the faculty lines they promised to give us three years ago?

May 5, 2010
Ken Doyle
Hautman and Doyle Literary Agency
and Hemorrhoid Excision Center
141 West 27th Street
New York, NY 10001

Dear Ken,

Do you know what you've unleashed, making a six-figure sale for Vivian Zelles? Every student novelist I've ever known—along with a few I've never met—is tracking me down to remind me of the halfhearted praise I once bestowed on his or her work. The ones who still live here in town are dropping by with their cherubic infants and jars of homemade jam. Some of them, I suspect, haven't written so much as a greeting card for years, but the news of Vivian's sale is like blood in the water, and now, fins sparkling, into the shallows they come.

I'm sure the bold and the brash will contact you directly, but if you're curious about who's been vetted, the only two I can safely vouch for at this moment are Eileen Tolentino and Carlos DaFoy. I won't bother to describe their work—you obviously make your own decisions—except to say that Tolentino's prose will be more palatable if you can get her to quit with the obsessive renditions of bodily functions; and DaFoy (a restless, bearded man with the tics and gesticulations of a hopping spider) ought to admit to himself that he's a writer of historical romance and start collecting his checks. You'll see if there's anything you can do for them. As for the others: I don't like homemade jam.

Ken, in your e-mail from last week you asked how Browles was doing. I assumed the question was pro forma (or a further opportunity for you to rub salt in the wound)—until yesterday evening when Janet called to tell me what I now conclude you already knew: that HRH gave an interview. His first in nine years. Not to *The New York Times,* thank god, or *The Paris Review,* but to *Avenue A,* an online journal, circulation five thousand. "I think you should read it," Janet said. She sent me the link.

"Still Writing After All These Years: A Conversation with H. Reginald Hanf." And what is Hanf, who has given almost no interviews in the past forty years, writing? *A Melville novel.* " 'I am interested in the conflation of contemporary and classic works,' Hanf says. 'And in the problem of *Bartleby* in particular.' " Is he fucking kidding? He lifted that phrase from Browles's proposal. I don't know if Browles reads *Avenue A*—I haven't seen him or spoken to him in the last few weeks—but some jackass will probably send him the link. Good god, Ken: HRH isn't going to write a *Bartleby* novel; a perusal of the interview immediately suggests that he's living on pabulum and stewed prunes, but because somebody showed up with a tape recorder (probably the day after he got the excerpt I sent him), he started regurgitating passages from Browles's book like a witless parrot. *But Browles doesn't know that.* He'll imagine Reg to be the potentate of old, the predictor of literary fortunes, and reading that interview is going to crush him. Do you remember HRH telling Janet that her writing was "sterile" and unproductive? She would kill me for telling you this, Ken, but that comment haunted her for years—it was like a venomous seed planted inside her, to the extent that when she couldn't get pregnant (she wanted children; I recognized myself as a poor candidate to be anyone's father), she felt he'd cursed her or created a weakness in her by issuing his verdict aloud. Years later when she found out about my affair (brief, unsatisfying, pointless), she was angry not only because of the betrayal but because of what she called my collusion with Reg. She claimed I had never disputed his diagnosis in regard to her work, that I was Reg's acolyte, his garden gnome, eager to believe in his pronouncements because of his preference for *Stain,* and in exchange for his favoritism—inspired mainly by prurience, she said—I was willing to sit back and see my friends and my classmates dismissed and degraded, ignored. She said I had bought into the idea, instilled in her by HRH, that she was a lesser writer than I was, and that she would never write anything good.

It was striking to realize that we were getting divorced at least in part because of something that had happened in a classroom two decades before—and even more striking, once the papers were signed, to admit to myself that, as vehement and strident as Janet was (and still is), I missed her. I have missed her terribly every day and have told her so (proclaiming my continued affection inadvertently once, in a public e-mail), but she claims she is healthier without me and remains unmoved.

Tolentino and DaFoy will send you their packets of prose next week. I was happy to hear that you got a nice arrangement for Troy at Folkstone. A bright spot in the fecund gloom of spring . . .

Drearily,
JTF

Carole—

You probably heard that I've been thoroughly scolded[*] for the LOR I wrote as a part of your application to Shepardville; once again, I'm sorry, I'm putting my ankles and wrists in the stocks and sending you a bushel of overripe tomatoes by campus post—you will find me publicly repenting of my sins on the quad. Does it alleviate your anger at all when I try to explain that my motives were good? If you'd applied to a school that deserved you, I would have written something more appropriately laudatory and banal.

Carole, I do hope you'll forgive me because I am in desperate need of a favor. I have one remaining graduate student, Darren Browles, the last of his kind, whose funding possibilities have gone up in flames. Rather than tucking his tail between his legs

---

[*] Janet was fully inflated with umbrage on your behalf, and I understand she wrote you a letter supplanting mine. Rest assured: despite the discomfitures of last fall, you can trust her. Yes, she's prickly, but she is also principled and well connected, and if you're determined to escape this World of Payne, she's well equipped to help you do so.

and leaving campus, he's been living on borrowed cigarettes and the castoffs from business school catered lunches; I suspect he sleeps and showers at the gym.

I recommended Browles to Bentham (Eleanor), which spurned him, and to Ken Doyle, my agent, who is so busy making millions off a comp lit student whose book I placed in his hairy hands that he can't devote even a few modest hours to this more demanding (i.e., less profitable) project. I even wrote to Zander Hesseldine and his kinky coterie about a summer RAship, but I got no response; they are probably busy packing their bags for Camp Foucault.

Worst of all—I hesitate to confess it—I sent a portion of Browles's manuscript-in-progress to my former advisor (I've told you about HRH) and it turns out he's babbling nonsense in a nursing home, having managed to emerge from the miasma of senescence long enough to spout the twisted and mistaken idea that he and not Browles is composing a novel based on Melville's *Bartleby the Scrivener*. Yes, I know, confidentiality! But in a moment of infirmity or nostalgia I was searching for wisdom and for the benefit of HRH's connections . . . The possibility of Browles's success appears to be receding over a distant horizon, but if he could get some summer funding and finally complete the damned book, he might still have a shot.

You have your fingers on the pulse of student finance over there in Gilbert; may I send Browles over? He's not in terrific shape right now, frankly—I'll give him a talking to about getting a haircut and changing his clothes—but when he doesn't feel the world is out to destroy him, he presents fairly well. I would so appreciate it, Carole. In the absence of other hidden pockets of funding, perhaps you could hire him to work in the office?

With a bow and an audible scraping noise,
Jay

Dear Dean Hinckler,

I have been tapped, once again and for reasons that defy human understanding, to write a letter—during the final crisis-ridden week of the semester—on behalf of my colleague Franklin Kentrell, who has nominated himself for chair of the university curriculum committee. Given your own recent, crucial work on the selection of dirges for the all-campus picnic, you may not have had time to grasp or appreciate the nature of Kentrell's contributions. He is, to put it mildly, insane. If you must allow him to self-nominate his way into a position of authority, please god let it be the faculty senate. There, his eccentricities, though they may thrive and increase, will at least be harmless. The faculty senate, our own Tower of Babel, has not reached a decision of any import for a dozen years.

By the by: word on the street is that our sociological friend, Ted Boti, despite various carrots dangled before him, will soon refuse to continue as chair. Rumors about his health have been circulating; through the pebbled glass of his office door, where one can observe him scratching the psoriatic tufts of hair on his head, he looks troubled and wan. A recommendation: next time you enlist someone from an outside department to step in and rule us, you should choose from the smaller and more disadvantaged units—Indigenous Studies or Hindi/Urdu, or some similarly besieged program, one of whose members, like a teenage virgin leaping into the bubbling mouth of a volcano, will sacrifice him- or herself in exchange for a chance that the larger community be allowed to survive.

As for Kentrell: he is one of the reasons no one wants to come near us. My suggestion to you: invent a committee for him— something Kafkaesque that requires years of fusty administrative investigation—and tell him that the difficult work he'll be putting in, until retirement, will free him from all other service, forever, amen.

Confident that my colleagues will join me in welcoming Kentrell's involvement in this distant and hypothetical realm, I remain

Yours in tender servitude,
Jay Fitger

May 20, 2010
USDA Forest Service
c/o Thomas Schaffler
Mailstop 1111
1400 Independence Avenue SW
Washington, DC 20250-1111

Dear Thomas Schaffler,

Simone Barnes, due to receive her BA in English in a matter of days (already the seniors can be found preparing for the upcoming pomp and ceremony by playing drinking games on the quad), has applied to your office in the hope of becoming an assistant wildlife observation specialist. Though I know almost nothing of the natural world—a blackbird and a robin are the same as far as I am concerned—it has fallen to me to recommend her.

Ms. Barnes has breathily informed me that should she be successful in this particular objective, she will immediately become "the happiest person on earth"—and on this basis alone I feel impelled to urge you to hire her.

I assume that sitting still for hours on a wooden platform, a pair of binoculars at the ready should anything ornithological raise its feathered head, would require steadiness, tranquility, and a meditative nature. Ms. Barnes—based on her performance in my Junior/Senior Creative Writing Workshop—manifests all three of these traits. A person of few words, she spent a good deal of her class time gazing languidly out the window. When called on, however, she demonstrated a reasonable familiarity with the subject at hand. She received a B+ as her final grade.

In case it's relevant, Ms. Barnes's final project was a whimsical piece of fiction about a young woman who lands a coveted job as an assistant wildlife observation specialist for the Forest Service. One day a beautiful young man ascends the platform on which she perches and, with no words exchanged (Ms. Barnes prefers narrative to dialogue), makes swooping love to her before transforming himself into a hawk and plunging, airborne, into the tree canopy, lustrous and green. The story conflated aspects of Rapunzel and Icarus and Leda's passionate swan—but confusions like these, given time and a healthy book list, can usually be alleviated, if not outright cured.

I can think of no other student better suited to the halcyon tasks Ms. Barnes will so delightedly embrace should you decide to hire her. Fortunate girl: to behold her ambitions still winking before her like stars.

Loftily,
Jay Fitger
Professor of Creative Writing and English
Payne University

Dear Carole,

Thank you for your letter. It was very kind. I wasn't sure whether anyone else on campus, now that we have entered the summer doldrums, would have seen the notice in the paper. I almost missed it myself. I don't always read the obituaries, though I suppose in another ten years that will be the page I turn to first, over morning coffee, for news of my friends.

I remember you telling me once that you counted it a good day, a promising day, when you skimmed the obits and found only notices for people over sixty-five. No babies, no college students, no teens. And you pointed out what should have been obvious: that in cases when the deceased is young, with no cause of death listed, the culprit is usually suicide or drugs.

With this letter I declare my intention to establish a scholarship in Darren Browles's name. I spoke briefly to his parents about it, as much as decency would allow a week after his death. They have two other children, one in college, and they have no money to spare—but I see no reason why they would oppose an honorific named for their son. Carole, I know you've secured your new job—off to the Big Ten; congratulations!—but I hope you can help me with this final task before you go. I confess that Browles's death has affected me severely, I am not in what you used to call "fighting form," and I don't want to spend loathsome hours battling the Kingdom of No in order to get this accomplished. The minimum to kick-start a scholarship, I understand, is $30,000. I'll take the money out of my savings and retirement. I have no reason to retire anyway.

The last time I saw Browles he told me he was working on his book again. We had run into each other at the drugstore and I was struck by the tremor of liveliness in his speech. He said he was revising for the nth time, and he made a point of telling me that there was a piece of advice I'd given him in class last fall that was useful to him, and I felt glad to have been useful. He made a joke about inscribing the final words of the novel, if he ever finished it, into the flat of his desk. And I remember thinking—because we were pacing back and forth between the pain relief and the vitamins—that he must have gotten a windfall of new meds to be feeling so well. But of course that's unfair.

You may want to know whether I told him about the HRH interview in *Avenue A*. In fact, I intercepted him a few minutes later on my way to the checkout, a collection of oddments tumbling in the plastic basket slung over my arm, with that purpose in

mind. I touched his shoulder and noticed his wide-set eyes—
one of them mildly strabismic—and a dried clot of saliva at the
corner of his mouth. *I was his advisor!* It was my job to encour-
age and critique and suggest, to help him see his own project as
if from a reader's point of view. And I needed to be honest with
him and to tell him that—regardless of my own machinations
on behalf of the program, and irrespective of any demented
remarks made by a formerly esteemed writer now poised at the
edge of an open grave—his novel was not very good; the light
of publication would not shine on the book in its current form.
But how to phrase that particular failure, which I knew was not
only Browles's, but mine? I clutched the sleeve of his jacket, the
rubber treadmill of the checkout rolling vertiginously at my side.
"Are you all right?" Browles asked. "Professor?"

He always called me "Professor"; I don't think he ever used
my name. And standing there by the checkout, still gripping
his jacket (the shoulder was torn, he probably couldn't afford a
new one), I saw him not as my only remaining graduate writing
student but in his own terms, Darren Browles-as-Browles, the
ding an sich.

Browles raised his arm as if to summon help, so I let go of his
sleeve and muttered something about a forgotten prescription.
And I walked away, telling myself that if he read the HRH interview he would quickly conclude that I had betrayed him; but at
some future moment he might also understand that I had been

trying, however ineffectually, to advocate for him and for other wannabe writers in the coming years.

As for the scholarship: I know that regulations and red tape thickly cover these things, but I would like to make this one as simple as possible. Call it the Darren Browles Memorial Fellowship, and let the interest pay out on a yearly basis to a student writer who, in no more than five hundred words, explains his or her artistic and financial need. My only other stipulation: there will be no letters of recommendation required or accepted. As long as I'm above ground, I'll read the applications, names redacted, and decide.

I suppose this is the last letter of recommendation anyone will write for poor Browles, so let me say this about him. Socially, he was awkward—shy, I suppose—and his writing at times was subpar; but an idea had presented itself to him, knocking at his brain like a nighttime traveler, and instead of shutting the door in its face, Browles built it a fire, he drew a chair for it up to the hearth and spent half a decade trying to decipher and then convey what it struggled to tell him. He was patient and industrious and quietly determined. Buffeted by setbacks and rejection and his own limitations, he persevered. Furthermore, he was kind—an admirable person. I wish I had told him these things directly, rather than saving my praise of him for letters and e-mails sent to other people: a correspondence Browles would never benefit from or see.

One thing the obituary didn't mention: he burned his work. He wiped six drafts of the novel off his computer and made a bonfire of the paper copies in an outdoor fire pit behind his apartment. He apparently explained as much to his family, in a note. "He said he didn't want us to read what wasn't finished," his mother told me when we spoke on the phone. She asked if I'd read the book, and if it was good, and I told her it was.

Thanks for your attention to the scholarship, Carole. And thanks (in advance) for shielding me from the talons of the development office. Explain to them that I have not won the lottery, I did not inherit from an eccentric millionaire great-aunt, and I am not an ardent booster of this institution. (They ought to know that by now: I believe my reputation precedes me.) This is my one and only bequest, and it springs not from tenderness toward my employer but from belated love and admiration for Browles.

Let me know what other information you need, and I'll try to get it to you ASAP, before you leave town and before the new semester begins. Though we in English are still in limbo as regards our new chair (Boti is AWOL, perhaps holed up in a cave with a pointed spear), we've been told that the heavy construction on the building will be finished this fall. In fact, yesterday I spotted an asthmatic Shakespearean and two balding Modernists, presumably ejected from the architecture building, ferrying their books and bits and bobs across the quad, a little ragtag caravan of refugees returning to their long-lost home. While the economists will wait until the fleurs-de-lis have been inscribed by master carvers on their office doors, we in English will probably spend another few months wearing hazmat suits and latex gloves. To wit: this morning, a workman politely knocked at my door to warn me about an orange electrical cord in the hallway—he didn't want me to trip—but he neglected to mention that three feet beyond the electrical cord was a large receptacle sporting a sign marked WARNING: ASBESTOS.

Mourning your departure already,
J.

P.S.: I'm sure you know that I'll miss you terribly, having no other ex-girlfriends and only one resentful ex-wife here on campus. I understand that you don't want to stay in touch, and I'll respect that decision. Have you selected the lucky person on whom I'll bestow my recommendations, once you leave office?

Ballot for Election to the Faculty Senate—please return to the office of Dean Philip Hinckler by July 11, 2010.

You may vote for up to three candidates for the Faculty Senate. Place an X by the names of the faculty for whom you vote. Faculty Senate members serve a (renewable) term of three years.

_____   Winifred Matchett (Sociology)

_____   Klaus Arthursen (German, Scandinavian, and Dutch)

_____   R. T. Sawma (Computer Science)

_____   Philip Lang (Psychology)

_____   Miriam Schoellner (History)

_____   Phoebe Allan (Philosophy)

__X__   Franklin Kentrell (English)

(Electronic Signature and Department or Unit)
J. Fitger
Creative Writing/English

Eleanor Acton, Director
Bentham Literary Residency Program
P.O. Box 1572
Bentham, ME 04976

Dear Eleanor,

The purpose of this letter is to recommend warmly to you a former student, Max Wylie-Hall, for a one-month writer's residency (January, please) at Bentham. Max completed his undergraduate degree here five years ago (English and anthropology), finishing up cum laude with a 3.8. During his final semester in my fiction workshop he wrote a competent but lethargic story about a sellout who—though he once had dreams and aspirations—finds himself at thirty years old (gasp!) with two ungrateful adenoidal children and a corporate job. The worst fate some undergrads can imagine for themselves: full employment, a home, a spouse and kids, a car.

So: I was surprised to find a thinner and darkly mustached version of Mr. Wylie-Hall at my office door half a decade later and even more surprised to read the new work he pressed on me. *Exquisite prose:* he has a bit of a Faulkner fixation, but that will probably resolve itself—do take a look. Wylie-Hall tells me that during the past five years he has held a series of menial jobs (warehouse, restaurant, lawn service, etc.) that allowed him an artist's flexible schedule as well as the peace of mind that comes of self-abnegation. I don't know that he'll finish the book he's working on, but I'd like to give him the opportunity to try. No caveats or warning flags: Wylie-Hall is stolid and serious and will not spend his free time scoping out opportunities for debauchery. He wants to write.

Thank you for your thoughtful letter and generous check for the Darren Browles Memorial Fellowship. I gather Janet told you. She showed up at my apartment a few weeks ago (she actually cut a vacation short and came back to Payne when she heard the news), washed the dishes that had collected in my sink, swept and squeegeed my floor, and then set two generous glasses of whiskey on the yellow enamel-topped kitchen table (one of my souvenirs from the divorce; she didn't want it), where we sat and talked late into the night. I felt as if the past ten years had been folded up like a battered tent between us, and it was only by exerting extreme self-control that I refrained from inviting her, at least for one night, to move back in.

You aren't the only person to suggest that I identified with Browles, that I saw him as an earlier and more ingenuous version of myself. It's a reasonable thesis but I resist it, as it posits Browles as a concept more than a person—a screen upon whom others cast their wishful light.

He deserved better.

Lately I've been puzzling over the way in which HRH, on a weekly basis during the Seminar, somehow persuaded us that he wielded inordinate power over our futures, that he could predict and even determine who would flounder and who would succeed. Shame on us that we often believed him. And for following his counsel rather than my conscience, shame on me. (None of the above should be mistaken for an apology, by the way; my apology to you, twenty-some years in coming, will arrive by separate cover, accompanied by a modest donation to Bentham.)

Onward. Your plan for a "reunion weekend" at Bentham in October has a poignant appeal: Madelyne TV would have loved the idea and been the first to sign up; and Janet has a brother in New Hampshire (an unbearable prig, but every year or two she feels obliged to see him); and you've already got Troy tidily tucked in his lakeside cabin; so it's only a matter of persuading Ken—tell him to write it off as a business expense and round up some new clients. But I'll have to decline. It turns out October will be busy for me, first because of the folderol reopening of the building in which English resides (long story—you don't want to hear it); and second because, defying common sense as well as my own and my colleagues' best interests, I have decided to accept a desperate departmental nomination for chair. Janet will tell you that, throughout this institution, I am widely disliked. (I'm sure you're shocked at the news.) She has attempted to bolster me, however, by claiming that, though understandably reviled, I am not universally distrusted, and on that basis I should serve out a three-year term. Last week she went so far as to smuggle into my office a contraband letter of nomination[*] written by the acting chair, Ted Boti, who recommended, in sweeping and hyperbolic language, that I take his place. The poor misguided soul described me as generous, "a champion for the department and particularly its students"; he went on to say that my disagreeable nature was "at least 50 percent façade" and that "Fitger behaves like more of an ass than he actually is." Janet described these comments as persuasive praise.

Still, both the administration and I remained wary, even after receiving the news—shocking to one and all—that my colleagues in English unanimously supported my nomination. Even then I was tempted to refuse, but three facts argued for my installation: 1. because of recent departures and abdications, and because nearly half our faculty are now ineligible underpaid adjuncts, there is no other qualified and willing candidate; 2. my literary career, if not dead, is at a profound and dismal standstill (just ask Ken about this when you see him); and 3. the

---

[*] How did Janet, an admissions officer in the law school, acquire a copy of Boti's letter, you ask? It pains me to say so, but it appears that my ex-wife is now dating the dean.

condition and morale of the department can't get any worse. Hence: I agreed. And it appears that the month of October will be chockablock with bureaucratic amusements and festivities I'm not free to turn down.

I wish we had thought to schedule a reunion before.

You asked me point-blank about Troy. I'm not surprised to hear he's become an ascetic (though I hadn't pictured the uncooked food and the sandals); he must look like a seer, and I suppose the Bentham literary pilgrims are eagerly gathering each evening, lotus position, by his cabin door. But the truth? No, Troy never read me his work during any late-night phone conversations. We never spoke by phone, and I have no idea what he's writing, or if he's writing at all.

So sue me, I lied. But you probably suspected me of doing so, and you invited Troy regardless. You and I are both in the business of believing in, and promoting, things that don't yet exist. The leap of faith: it's equal parts wishful thinking, vicarious ambition, and bullshit, and yet . . . I can already envision the moment when I open Troy's new book and find within it, among the acknowledgments, your name and mine; and we both know how beautiful the book will be, how clearly it will speak to something within us—some previously unarticulated thought or reflection that, once recognized, we will never want to be without again.

Enjoy the summer, Eleanor. Fall will arrive soon enough, with requests from students trickling in via e-mail, and the trees that shade Willard Hall flushing red at the hem. There is nothing more promising or hopeful than the start of the academic cycle: another chance for self-improvement, for putting into practice what one learned—or failed to learn—during the previous year.

Forgive the length of this letter. Next time I will try to send you a shorter one.

In the meantime I hope once again to consider myself
Your friend,
Jay

Acknowledgments

I'm very grateful to my editor, the marvelous Gerald Howard, and to Jeremy Medina, Amy Ryan, Emily Mahon, and Nicole Pedersen at Doubleday. Chocolate and flowers to Lisa Bankoff (who was very patient with my limited understanding of the cell phone) and to Daniel Kirschen at ICM.

To the Rockefeller Bellagio Center: I'll be indebted forever for the gift of a residency in spring 2011.

Thanks to Lawrence Jacobs, world's most enthusiastic and supportive spouse, who read the first draft of this book and said, "I'm glad we have different last names."

As for Emma and Bella who, defying logic, seem not to have tired of my quirky sense of humor: here's to you two crazy weasels, with thanks and love.

About the Author

Julie Schumacher's first novel, *The Body Is Water*, was an ALA Notable Book of the Year and a PEN/Hemingway Award finalist. Her other books include a short story collection, *An Explanation for Chaos*, and five books for younger readers. She lives in St. Paul and is a faculty member in the Creative Writing Program and the Department of English at the University of Minnesota.